The Short Story Press Collection

Sasha Hanton

The Short Story Press
Collection

CONTENTS

Broken 7

Cyber Loss 9

Don't Need Recipies 14

Extra Strength 19

Gin No Tonic 21

Dreams 26

Normal Week 27

Doll 29

Witches Brew 32

My Own Coffin 36

Ginger Vampires 44

Season of Blood 50

Witches Hollow 57

CONTENTS

Just as the stories foretold 68

Only Luck 70

Werewolf Road Trip 73

Train to Nowhere 78

Prayer Power 82

Traitor 85

Fae Feast 87

The Wood 91

Leap of Faith 95

Emerald Hills 98

Burn 101

Branded 106

Burn The Witch 108

Balloon in the Sky 110

Falling 112

Battered Old Photograph 114

Troth 116

CONTENTS

Primal 118

Anxiety 120

Rules 122

Ephemeral 125

The Chant 138

It All Started With A Letter 140

Blood Stained Carpet 143

Twisted Love 145

High Tide 147

Wolves in Human Clothing 149

Dyed Red 152

One Night 155

Two-Faced 160

The Short Story Press Collection
Copyright© Sasha Hanton 2023

ISBN: 978-0-6452889-2-6
Publisher: Dragon Sisters

Dedication

For my family, who, for all the years I have been writing, have always supported me
and believed in my potential.

This would not have been possible without them.

How The Short Story Press Collection Came to Be

I started my blog *the short story press* back in December 2013, almost ten years ago, I was fresh out of university and still deciding what to do with myself. It started as a place for me to post short stories and practice my craft, then slowly over time it turned into a blog where I shared events in my life, it's played host to travel stories and special event pieces along with posts about the general chaos of life. *The short story press* no longer exists as I changed my website to *sashahanton.com* in September but through this collection the early days of my blog will always live on.

For years I kept it active with two short stories a week; Saturday Word of the Day and Wednesday Prompt Smash, over time those trickled off as life became more demanding, but I still post a few times a year and I've recently begun posting semi-regularly again by bringing back the Wednesday Prompt Smash.

In 2017, I was celebrating the acceptance of my story *Dealt in Sin* being accepted to be published in the *Beginnings Anthology.* I decided to take another step forward with my writing and put together a collection of my own short stories for publication; so *The Short Story Press Collection* came to be as an eBook. It contained stories pulled from the blog, edited, and expanded on, along with original stories not to be found anywhere else. Those original stories are in this new edition of *The Short Story Press Collection*, along with more new material and other stories from the blog that it finally felt right to expand and edit.

This version of the collection contains the segment *A Touch of Fantasy*, in 2017 when I first put together the collection I chose to leave out the more fantastical stories I'd been considering putting in as they didn't meld well with the collection as a whole – those stories are still not in here – but as I put together this collection I knew I had to include a few with fantasy leanings as I am for the most part a fantasy writer these days.

When I started the blog in 2013, I'd ping between different genres fairly frequently as I was still honing my craft, and discovering who I was as a writer. The journey of discovery never really ends but I'm more confident in my skills these days and when people ask me what I write more often than not I say "fantasy", other answers include "urban fantasy, but I'm hoping to try high fantasy soon" or "speculative fiction". Sometimes I'll still find myself dipping a toe into science fiction, or on the odd occasion, I might contemplate writing more literary fiction. Fantasy is where my heart is so this time around it absolutely had to be a part of the collection.

I've also included some more transitionary pieces to lead from one segment to the next, giving the collection itself a more natural flow, although considering they are all short stories you are more than welcome to simply pick and choose which ones you'd like to read.

My goal with bringing the collection to print now is to keep a link to my start with short stories, they have done so much for me even as I now tend to focus more on writing complete novels. This collection also serves as a reflection; it contains pieces from the early days of *the short story press* alongside stories freshly written, it commemorates ten years of my writing. If you read carefully, you might just be able to tell which pieces are older and which are newer by the slight changes in style and tone from my growth as a writer. Or perhaps you won't be able to tell any difference, perhaps guessing what's from the early 2010s to what's from 2023 is an impossible task because as far as you can tell my writing just shifts and changes all over the place (or hasn't changed a lick).

I hope the collection contains something for you, for every reader; a story that you enjoy deeply, resonates with you, inspires a creative spark, and provides some comfort or a deep train of thought. There are so many stories contained within, some that are extremely different from each other and some that ring with the same feeling, stories that (I hope) bring visuals to life in the mind's eye and stories that stir recollections of feelings, those written in first person to those in the third person. Amongst them, I truly do hope there's at least one you love, that might tempt you to read it again when the time is right.

If you enjoy the collection please leave me a review, whether it is a lengthy written review or a simple star rating. I appreciate every little bit of your support and it truly does help. I encourage you to leave reviews for all your favourite books, especially those by indie publishers and authors.

Happy reading,
Sasha Hanton
November 2023

With A Twist

Broken

I thought I wanted to know. I thought knowing would make things better, but it just made everything worse.

For the longest time, I'd wanted to know what was wrong with me, why my family had abandoned me and why the world shunned me. I just wanted to feel normal. I thought if I could just figure this out then I would be able to move past it and be normal. How wrong I was.

Now here I lay. Broken. Unable to say anything. Speechless, and scared of what I have learnt. Of all the possible reasons that I had imagined my family leaving me, of all the quirks that I had, never in a hundred thousand years could I have thought of this.

Truth is far stranger than any fantasy. There is no undoing what I have learnt... although maybe that isn't altogether true given my circumstances. I wish I could cry. Spread out on this cold surface I feel as if I have lost everything.

I'd just wanted answers. Had it been so wrong to want to know my origins? For a moment I consider what if I hadn't wanted this, what if I hadn't persisted? But I realise it's a silly thought- what's done is done.

My eyes linger on my left arm, it has been disconnected from me - all of my parts have been disconnected. When I came here I sealed my own fate. In order to keep the truth I had learned hidden, they had broken me.

As soon as they had begun breaking me the truth had become apparent. I was not normal. I wasn't even human, what a joke. After spending my life as an orphan and just wanting to be a normal person, it turns out I wasn't anything - just a machine, an AI programmed to feel human and integrate with humanity.

Once I knew the truth I was a risk. They couldn't have such risks running loose in the world. And so, here I am. Broken into pieces on a metal slab, my cognitive processor still active but all other functions disabled - for the most part, disassembled.

Cyber Loss

Left, right, dodge, kick, swerve.
Block, twist, sweep the leg, run.
Run, run, run.
Keep running, don't stop.
Cough, wheeze, push through.
Jump, climb, drop... crash.

-

Slugger, it hurts.
Can't see a damn thing.

-

All of a sudden there's a feeling like my head's being ripped off and unexpectedly there's light.

"Welcome back, how was it?"

Where in the hell is that voice coming from?

"Turn your head a little to the left please, that's better. Now tell me, how was it?"

My eyes are still adjusting to the light, but I can just make out a feminine silhouette. Where am I?

"Eh-hem, would you at least say something?" the silhouette moves so I can make out that her hands are now on her hips.

"Who are you?" I manage to squeak out the words, though my throat feels dry.

"Goodness, really? Jeez, they promised they'd sorted out the mild memory loss issue." The silhouette does not seem impressed and starts moving forward. As she approaches, my eyes adjust to pick-up details and the silhouette comes into form. "Would you please not stare, it's rather rude."

Even if she says not to stare, how could I possibly not?

In front of me stands what could be considered a regular female from afar but up close there's no mistaking it, she's a robot. The chest area is rounded but only on the sides, in the middle is an open compartment showing off a bright green battery core.

"I asked you not to stare." The robot pulls her arms over her chest to hide the energy core, "Please I'm here to assist you. Sir, if you were not currently experience a spell of memory loss you'd never be ogling my battery so."

Looking up at the robot's face her cheeks seem, strangely enough, to be tinged lemonade pink.

"Who are you?" I ask again.

"I'm Delta, sir." The robot retreats a few steps back from me. "You came here to trial equipment for my creator."

"Who's your creator? How do I know them?" I have to cough a bit to clear my throat but I manage to get out a few questions.

"I'm not allowed to call him anything other than my creator so I cannot inform you, but I will take you to him now if you'd like." I nod in response and the robot swivels her body around and begins to glide forward. I'm marginally confused as she has legs, yet as I look down I notice that in the place of feet are a set of wheels.

It takes a moment for me to get up from the floor. But it seems that besides a bit of memory loss, whatever it was that I was doing didn't affect my body or motor functions. As I jog to catch up with Delta I notice how barren the room is, with its blank white walls and lack of furnishings.

The walk is silent and long. Wherever we are it's big and has a lot of twists and turns.

After following Delta for what must have been an hour or more, we finally reach our destination.

"One moment please," Delta holds her wrist up to a scanner and the huge set of security doors before us slowly begin to open, "you may go through now. My creator shall be inside waiting for you."

"Thanks," I mumble, trying not to stare at the robot, before I walk past and through the doors.

Inside, the room is sparse. There's a huge projector screen and in front of it, there's a massive chair with the back turned to me. But I don't see anyone.

I walk towards the chair but before I'm even halfway it swivels around, revealing a smug looking man. At first, I don't recognise him... but then I look a little harder and it snaps into place.

This man, Delta's creator, is none other than Dr Emerick Dulse. With this revelation I feel more confused than ever, why would I ever agree to test his creations?

"Officer Melten, so how was it?"

I don't know how to answer, I still don't even know what I was testing... or how I even got here.

"What am I doing here?" I decide to get some answers rather than to answer him.

"Uh, oh, yes I see. Oh, that is too bad, hmm yes. No, that should work." He doesn't seem to have heard my question and instead seems to be speaking to himself. Then he looks at me and grins.

"Not to fret Officer Melten, we'll just give your memory a jog and it'll all be peachy. Terribly sorry it seems my assistants forgot to finish the disengage code for the neural connectivity which has triggered a small touch of memory loss. As I said though, you just need a little jolt and it'll all come back nice and clear."

I take a step back not liking the sinister grin on the doctor's face.

"Now, now Officer Melten please, trust me." Rising from his chair Dr Dulse approaches me.

"Stay back, I might not know why I'm here but I do know that you're a twisted psycho who's wanted for crimes against humanity." Instinctively I take another step back.

"Fine, fine, have it your way Officer Melten. I don't need to be close to jog your memory, I just need to find the correct words... hmm, now let's see." The doctor stays in place, pondering something. I fight the urge to turn heel and run, not that I'd even know how to get out of this place.

"Uh yes, that should do nicely." Dr Dulse sets his eyes on me. "Officer Melten, how did you find your testing of the virtual reality headgear? I trust that you found it passing? And that you were able to observe that my robotic helper Delta is within the standard guidelines for robotics?"

I'm about to rebut that I don't know what he's talking about as a searing pain rips through my head. It's like a sudden migraine, and it completely debilitates me. I find myself falling to my knees, screaming in agony at the splitting head pain. And then, as quickly as the pain came on, it disperses and my memories come flooding back to me.

The reason I'm here is because my task force, which was meant to be bringing the doctor in, needed to gather actual evidence that there were issues with the technology Dr Dulse was creating. Upon raiding his lab we'd been disappointed to find that from all standpoints his robots did seem to fall within guidelines, albeit just barely - they were after all distinguishable from humans. The doctor, who had been quite pleased with our disappointment, offered me the chance to test out a few of his newest inventions, I begrudgingly agreed as it held the possibility of discovering evidence of misconduct.

As all of this came rushing back, I felt crushed. Yes, his virtual reality headgear had a major fault, but apparently, that was being corrected... and it wasn't out on the market yet, so I couldn't charge him with that.

"Well, all clear now, Officer Melten?" Dr Dulse's voice sounded incredibly smug to my ears.

"All clear. Currently your VR gear can't be sold on the market yet, but as long as the memory issue is fixed it'll be fine... Now, if you don't mind Dr Dulse I need to report back to my squad."

"Of course. Oh, and Officer Melten please feel free to come back anytime." There was a smirk plastered across his face, if I wasn't a good officer I'd punch him.

"Don't think this means you're off the hook Dulse, we'll be watching you." With that said I left the building to report to my superiors how our investigation had been a bust.

"Creator he has now left the building and integrated himself into the unit."

"Thank you Delta, please see that the corpse is properly disposed of. It wouldn't do for anyone to find out we'd killed the real Officer Melten and replaced him with an android."

"Yes, of course, Creator. I'll have the assistance team drop the corpse into the battery fluid vat, which should properly disintegrate it."

"Yes, that'll do nicely Delta. Oh and Delta please restore yourself, we wouldn't want any of the investors to know you're a robot."

Don't Need Recipies

Taylor loved food; unfortunately, Taylor did not excel at cooking and would constantly be checking the recipe to see where he had gone wrong. It wasn't like Taylor was horrendous at cooking; it was just that he preferred doing other things. Of course, those other things usually involved eating. Because cooking his own meals was cheaper than going somewhere, Taylor had acquired a large collection of recipe books.

As it were Taylor's life was about to change, unbelievably so. It commenced on a misty Tuesday. A man with a big top hat arrived at Taylor's door and rang the bell twice.

Bring, Bring

Taylor was in the kitchen, bemoaning his terrible luck as the soufflé he'd been trying to make deflated in front of his eyes. Nobody ever visited Taylor, and if they did they certainly never rang the doorbell. Dejected from another culinary failure Taylor dragged himself to the front door.

Upon the opening of the door the top hat man smiled. Tilting the hat up, he revealed his face to Taylor. The moustache bothered Taylor, he didn't like moustaches. He fixed the stranger with a scrutinizing look, mainly exhibiting his dislike of the moustache by glaring at the man's upper lip. The stranger's smile widened.

"Taylor my boy, how are you?"

Eyes still fixed on the moustache Taylor replied.

"Fine thank you. Now please tell me who exactly you are and what you are doing here."

"I'm your uncle Frederick of course, Taylor, my boy. Didn't you get my letter? I'm here to take you home."

Taylor eyed the moustache with doubt, as far as he knew, he had no home other than his apartment and no family that were alive. With his mother's death last fall, all of his relatives were gone to his knowledge. And as for a letter, he didn't really bother checking his mail unless it was a bill because those were important.

"I don't read letters, and I don't have any living family. Now good day sir."

Slamming the door in the stranger's face and then promptly locking it Taylor resolutely marched to the kitchen to start on another recipe.

"Now Taylor, my boy, that wasn't very nice. Come along we must be getting you home."

Taylor practically jumped at the sudden voice, he turned around and sure enough the moustache was there. Now please note, it was not the strange man behind Taylor but simply his moustache. And if a moustache had eyes it would have been staring at the recipe book in Taylor's hand.

"Best put that book down lad. Where we're going, we don't need recipes."

Taylor shakily put the book down, and that's when, all of a sudden, the moustache jumped onto him and the floor seemed to slip away.

"Aah!" Taylor screamed as they began plummeting - though there was no discernible bottom so they weren't really plummeting towards anything. This was not how today was meant to be thought Taylor staring down at the blackness.

"Cheer up Taylor, my boy." Decreed the moustache through the darkness, "We're almost there!"

"Where exactly are you taking me?" cried out Taylor, still perturbed about being forcefully taken from his recipe books.

"Home, my boy, I'm taking you home." Taylor slumped, well the closest thing to slumping when one is falling down a deep dark chasm.

This was utterly crazy; he was being abducted by a moustache for goodness sake!

"Why is this happening to me?" moaned Taylor.

"Here it is! Look out below!" Taylor heard the moustache shout, and looking down could see a strange marshmallow kind of thing.

Within seconds they were landing on the marshmallow thing, which was incredibly soft and squishy. Hungry for a snack and curious about this large, landing pad Taylor tore off a piece and popped it in his mouth.

"Mmm, that's a good marshmallow."

"Taylor! It is incredibly rude to eat part of the city's infrastructure." The moustache addressed him; if it had eyes it would have been glaring at him.

"Yeah well, you kidnapped me and ruined my soufflé."

"Come now Taylor, let's not label things unnecessarily. Please, let's just be getting on to the house. The family is waiting for you."

Taylor grumbled in response and followed the moustache; it wasn't like he could get back to his apartment anyway. As he walked he began to wonder about this so-called family.

"You say the family is waiting, are they all moustaches too?"

"Now don't be absurd Taylor, once we get home you'll see."

There was no more conversation after that; Taylor passed time by observing his surroundings. Most of the buildings seemed to be made of food products. And oddly enough there were no people or even animals to be seen. Taylor found himself wondering if he'd somehow taken drugs or gotten concussed because surely this was a hallucinogenic dream.

"This is it, open the door will you please." Taylor was shocked out of his thoughts by the moustache's sudden words. Looking ahead he saw a door made from what appeared to be waffles in front of him. Grasping the large lollipop doorknob Taylor turned it to be greeted by a cacophony of noise, and then standing there in front of him was his mother.

"Welcome home, son."

Well, that settled it then, Taylor thought. If his mother who had passed away last fall was standing here in front of him, well there was only one reasonable answer. He was dead.

"Taylor? Are you okay, sweetie? You look pale." His mother fussed about as she ushered him inside.

"The boy's fine, Vanessa. Probably just a tad shook up, first time travelling through dimensions and all that." The moustache bounded past them, "Now, look, he'll settle once he's had a bit of a lie down, I should think."

"Do you think so, Frederick?" Taylor was still in shock. His feet were moving forward as his mother guided him into the house but he couldn't bring himself to say anything.

"Yes, Vanessa. Just let him get some rest." They'd wound up in a bedroom. Much like everything outside, all the furnishings were made from foods.

And that was it, as soon as he got into the bedroom Taylor found himself collapsing onto the bed and out like a light.

"Taylor? Darling?"

"Mum," Taylor mumbled, his eyes felt heavy, and his limbs sore.

'Yes, sweetie, I'm right here." A soft hand grasped his and another patted his forehead.

"Mum," He didn't want to open his eyes, this was surely a very pleasant dream and when he did open them his mother would be gone. But his eyes wouldn't stay shut.

"Are you feeling better, sweetie?"

"MUM!" Not a dream then, Taylor felt like fainting from shock but well that'd be a bit dramatic wouldn't it. "How are you here? How am I here? Am I dead?"

His mother chuckled at him and shook her head.

"Didn't you read Frederick's letter?"

"Whose letter?" The words left his mouth and then Taylor remembered the events of that morning, and the talking moustache.

"Your Uncle Frederick's letter, Taylor. Really, I thought you'd have a hard time forgetting him."

"You mean the moustache. You're trying to tell me that a moustache is my uncle."

"Well of course. It's not uncommon for a member of our kind to take on a simpler form, it's just that Frederick likes to be a moustache." That sent Taylor into a spin, none of this made any sense.

"Our kind? What does that even mean?" Taylor couldn't believe this was real, but there weren't many other options left.

"I'll tell you all about it. After you meet the rest of the family," His mother held her hand out for him.

Taylor wasn't sure what to do but finally ended up accepting her hand. No matter what this was, she was his mother and that had to mean something. She led him back through the house and into a living room.

"Everyone, this is Taylor." She said, nudging him forward. Taylor, was confused because there didn't appear to be anyone in the room just a bunch of knick-knacks.

"Hi, Taylor." But then, of course, the knick-knacks talked.

"Taylor, this is our family. I'm so glad you could finally be here and meet everyone!" His mother was beaming at him. But there comes a time when things are just too weird, and for Taylor this was it - so without saying a word he fainted on the spot.

-

Thick pillowy plumes of smoke wafted out of the apartment. The fire brigade had battled against the flames to evacuate the nearby apartments, but they couldn't reach the starting point of the fire.

It had been a gas leak, ignited by the stove top burner. The resident of the apartment couldn't be located, it was assumed he was dead and that the fragments of his body would be found amongst the ashes of the building.

Extra Strength

'It's hard being surrounded by superheroes, day in and day out. In the world where everyone is extraordinary, being a hero is ordinary, being a superhero that's the goal. Superheroes are more than extraordinary; they are above and beyond what anyone could ever hope to be.

So then how do superheroes become so super? How can they exist if it's so hard to become one?

That's easy, take SUPA Pills. SUPA- Strength Ultra Productive Activator Pills, they'll tap into your inner power and give you EXTRA STRENGTH!

Be a SUPA Hero!'

The holographic projector glitches as Mars Inferno is thrown through it, pixelating the iconic Captain Strong's face.

"Ugh," Mars Inferno grunts as she hits the wall.

"Hey!" Phobos Flame yells at The Demolisher, grasping his attention before he can go to finish off Mars Inferno. "Over here, you big dumb-dumb!"

As Phobos Flame distracts The Demolisher, Deimos Flare searches for something to help Mars Inferno. Deimos rifles through her bag searching until her hands grasp a plastic medicine bottle, she pulls it from the bag.

"I wasn't planning on taking these. I know you think they're dumb but not everyone is strong and brave like you Mars... and it's not like you can really judge - if I use these, I might be strong enough to save you, they could give me extra strength," Deimos mutters to Mars' unconscious form as she pops a few SUPA Pills into her mouth.

"Here goes nothing."

White, blinding, heat radiates from Deimos. It's like a wave of power coursing throughout her body, instinctively she can tell she's stronger now.

"Woah, I feel amazing!" Deimos cries out.

"Argh," Deimos is snapped out of her reverie when she hears Phobos' choked cry.

"OH right, in the middle of a fight. Hang on Phobos." With that, Deimos launches herself in the direction of The Demolisher projecting a stream of fire at him from her hands. "Take THAT!"

The flames like tentacles wrap around The Demolisher and Deimos feels relieved as his grip on Phobos releases. But the fire doesn't relent, it engulfs The Demolisher burning through the villain's costume and into his skin as the heat rises exponentially. As they continue to burn The Demolisher, small off-shoots of the flames tendril out licking up the walls and across the floors before starting to consume whatever they can.

Deimos quickly scurries over to where The Demolisher stands screaming in agony, pulling Phobos away from the fire in the nick of time. She drags her companion back to where Mars is lying on the ground unconscious, desperate to somehow keep them both out of the way of the flames.

"Oh lord, what have I done?" Deimos looks on in horror as her flames lick at the buildings, consuming everything in sight. Her lip quivers as The Demolisher's cries of torment fade to a whimper then vanish altogether leaving only the crackling of the fire. "This isn't what I meant to happen, I didn't want this, I... just wanted to be super."

Gin No Tonic

The knife protruded from the body like the murderer just didn't care about evidence. Then again, the knives had protruded from each of the bodies so far, nine in total- this one made ten. And yet it didn't make any sense, the murderer left behind the weapon and a nice set of fingerprints each time. Fingerprints that couldn't be found in any database. Not police records or hospital records.

It was like they didn't exist. No witnesses ever saw them, and no security footage had captured them. They were elusive. And if Toni didn't catch them soon that'd be it for her career as a detective, so this time Toni was praying for a miracle.

"Come on, a hundred and twenty people live in this building and nobody saw anything?"

"Sorry detective, but nobody's saying anything useful."

"Damn it." Toni was fuming as she waited for the evidence analysis. Their only new lead was a strand of hair - presumably human, and hopefully the murderer's.

-

The minutes ticked by like hours. Slow and excruciating. Why was it taking so long to get an analysis on a single strand of hair?

"Detective Gin?"

"Yes?"

"We've got your analysis results here, sorry it took so long." A mousy lab assistant handed Toni a stack of papers.

"All this? It was just a strand of hair."

"Well, uh, yes and uh no... y-you, see it, um, was, uh, rather strange... we've, uh, never seen anything like it. Anyway, um, I hope it can be of use in your investigation." The assistant stuttered a hurried goodbye before dashing back into the lab.

"Something they've never seen before, I wonder what that means?" murmured Toni exiting the corridor and heading to her office.

-

It was all gobbledygook as far as Toni was concerned; reading over the lab analysis was like trying to read upside down. Toni could make out the words but somehow couldn't make sense of it all. Each paragraph was more confusing than the last. About the only thing she'd been able to ascertain from the report was that the culprit had red hair-and something about its chemical composition was abnormal.

This wasn't making Toni's job any easier, red hair after all still meant a large suspect pool. It was then that her phone rang, she picked it up.

"Gin get to my office NOW!"

Toni gulped, the Chief wanted to see her.

-

Knock, Knock

"COME IN!"

Toni peeped her head around the door frame before fully entering the room.

"You wanted to see me, Chief?" Crossing her fingers behind her back, Toni prayed this wasn't what she thought it was.

"Yes, detective. I'm pulling you from the Serial Killings, got some smaller jobs for you."

"But Sir..." Toni protested, but the Chief fixed her with a hard glance, "can I at least ask why you're pulling me?"

"Detective Gin, you are being reassigned for your own safety. Data analysts have found a pattern in the victims, a pattern that shows you might be next..." With that said, the Chief slid the report across his desk. "Why don't you look over this data, I'm a bit busy to go into further detail. Just make sure you get these files back to me before you leave for the day, alright. Dismissed, Detective."

Picking up the report Toni left.

'Victim 1- Brown hair, blue eyes, 5'2, Caucasian. Name: Liza Trefelo.

Victim 2- Dyed pink hair, roots blond, green eyes, 5'7, African. Name: Delilah Warrant.

....

Victim 9- Red hair, brown eyes, 6'2, Caucasian. Name: Sid Le'Forge.

Victim 10- Blond hair, brown eyes, 5'4, Caucasian. Name: Thomas Trefelo.

....

Analysis of backgrounds of victims shows all attended Mountwood Middle School in 2078. All were members of the same class with teacher Mrs Hendbrige in their last year at the school. There were 20 students in that class, if the killer is a member of that class then there are 10 possible future victims including the teacher... not knowing who the killer is means there are 11 people of interest.

List of Students in Mrs Hendbrige's 2078 class:

Liza Trefelo

Thomas Trefelo

Vince Waterson

Delilah Warrant

Emmanuel Ford

April Olin

.....

Toni Gin'

It was all there in the report. The connection between the victims.

"God damn it, I should have spotted this... I should have remembered their names. Christ, I went to school with them..." Right there in the middle of the police headquarters hallway it all clicked into place.

"I'm a person of interest, a potential future victim... I need to, I need to..." need to what? It wasn't like she could leave town, that would be suspicious. And she already had her gun, so it wasn't like she needed to get something to protect herself.

What exactly was it that she needed to do?

All these thoughts were running through Toni's head as she collided with a passer-by on the way to her office. The collision knocked Toni and the passer-by onto the ground, scattering the report papers around them.

"Sorry," Toni apologised as she gathered together the papers she'd been reading.

The person she'd collided with said nothing, they got up and stood there silently. As Toni rose to her feet , she noticed the demented grin on the stranger's face and the shocking burgundy red colour of their hair.

Instinctively she took a step back as her hand went to the holster on her hip, but before she could pull out her gun they charged at her. They looked weak but clearly, that wasn't the case as they tackled Toni to the ground, the wind was knocked out of her. In a matter of minutes, they were straddling Toni's waist and their hands were clawing at her. Toni twisted in place, trying her hardest to keep the stranger from pinning her down. She could feel the adrenaline in her body and using what strength she could muster bucked the attacker off her.

Her attacker unseated Toni wasted no time in scrambling across the floor and rising to her feet. While the stranger was still dazed and lying on the ground, she made a dash for her office. However she was buffeted back by an invisible force.

Unable to escape, she turned her back to the invisible wall. The stranger got up slowly, sniggering as their eyes locked on Toni once more.

"Silly, little mouse, thinks it can escape." A demented laugh followed the words, but Toni wasn't going down without a fight.

BANG She unholstered her gun and shot a round into the air. The stranger was unfazed. A dreadful thought entered Toni's mind, if she couldn't get out then those outside couldn't get in, there would be no aid.

While she was thinking the attacker lunged forward. She was expecting the attack, but even as she went to dodge it occurred to her how much faster the stranger was. They hadn't managed to tackle her down, but they had off-set her balance. To avoid falling as the stranger spun round to attack her once more, Toni grabbed a handful of their hair.

"Owwww!" Howled the stranger as Toni wrenched a few strands out. In her hand the hair felt strange, almost like metal, but Toni had no time to consider it as the stranger launched at her once more.

She couldn't dodge them this time as they tackled her to the ground wrestling the gun from her hands.

Their positioning kept her from being able to reach for her gun as it was thrown across the floor. The stranger erratically began clawing at her once more. When for some reason they paused their clawing and moved their hands away, Toni thought she saw an opening. But as she went to buck them off, she was the one caught by surprise as their right hand slapped her across the cheek and their left hand revealed a knife.

She rolled to the left as the attacker plunged the knife down to her right, then as they yanked it up she attempted to once more buck them off her.

"Uh-uh, none of that." Alas, they were prepared for her attempt and instead, their grin extended across their face.

"Time for your investigating to end," laughed the stranger, as they brought down the knife for the final time.

Dreams

There's water all around me, I'm underneath it and yet I can breathe. I try to swim but it seems I am fixed in place, I can see sunlight coming from above so I must not be too deep.

For a while, there's nothing but the water, and then suddenly something slams into the water. Whatever it is must be heavy as it plummets quickly downward. As it rockets past me, I'm horrified to see a human hand and some wisps of hair...

I startle from my sleep, sweat upon my forehead. Looking around I know I'm at home, safe in bed, but I can't shake the fear that my dream filled me with. I fumble for the lamp on the nightstand and click it on. The light makes me feel a little better but my skin is covered in goose-bumps - what was that dream about? Whose body was it?

The next day at work a call comes in, there's a girl missing. People from all around town volunteer to help search for her. We in the police force create a search perimeter and start looking. All day nothing can be found, that is until we dredge the lake and find her body weighed down at the bottom.

Normal Week

"Cassandra, what did you want to discuss so urgently? We're not scheduled for another session till next month."

"Dr.Andrews, things feel wrong."

"Wrong? Whatever do you mean Cassandra? What's happened to you recently?"

"It has been a normal, boring week, but something just isn't right. I don't know what it is, I just can't put my finger on it but I know something is wrong."

"Try breaking down your week. Perhaps if you examine it in detail you'll find your answer."

"What's to examine? It was normal! I woke up on Monday and went to work, same on Tuesday, Wednesday and every other day of the week. On Friday I went for after work drinks and on Saturday I stayed home because it was my day off."

"And on Sunday?"

"On Sunday, on Sunday... on Sunday I saw Jay."

"You saw Jay?"

"Yeah, I saw Jay. Jay had come over to see me... wanted to talk about how we left things."

"Cassandra, do you realise what you are saying?"

"I know, I know, Jay is bad for me. I know, every time I get involved with Jay it gets toxic, but Jay's just so hard to resist and I know it's detrimental to my recovery but I just can't resist Jay-"

"Cassandra!"

"Wh-what?"

"Jay is dead, Cassandra, you know this. You can't have seen Jay because Jay is dead."

"N-no but, but I saw Jay. I saw Jay on Sunday, we talked, we had sex, we..."

"I'm going to prescribe you an anti-hallucinogen, you're slipping Cassandra... and here I thought you were making such progress with your recovery."

Doll

She came in from the rain, clothes clinging to her skin, water droplets beaded in her hair like tiny translucent pearls. There's a wild, humorous gleam in her eyes as she shakes her head spraying water across the room.

"What a rush!" She crows practically skipping as she makes her way to settle down in front of the fire. "It's absolutely bucketing out there."

"What were you doing outside?" It's the obvious question, but she waves it off as she peels the first wet layer of clothing from her body.

"I wonder how long it'll rain for; do you think it'll still be raining this time tomorrow?"

"I'm not sure." A moment of silence. I avert my eyes as she flings her shirt across the room, listening for the wet thud as it lands on the floorboards. "Why do you want to know? You're not going out again, are you?"

She ignores that question too, glossing over it as she stands naked waiting for the fire to dry her off. "I love the rain, don't you? It's so refreshing."

It'll flood the garden if it keeps up, drown my preciously cultivated herbs. That's a far cry from refreshing in my books.

"I don't mind it, but I wouldn't be heading out in this weather." I shuffle awkwardly across the room, keeping my eyes on the floor and moving sideways like a crab. "What were you doing out there in the first place?"

"Oh boo, you can't be cooped up indoors all the time. Won't go out in the rain, won't come out in the snow, next you'll be saying there's no reason to ever go outside." She ignores my question again; I don't know why I was expecting anything different.

"I'm not that boring. It's perfectly fine going outside in light rain, or when the sun is out, even a little snow isn't a problem." I mumble, she probably can't hear me. "I just don't see the point in going out when there's a blizzard or it's bucketing down."

There's a bathrobe and a towel hanging on the bedroom door, I scoop them into my arms before shuffling back the way I came.

"Not everyone is as reckless as you, it's dangerous going out in this weather." This time I speak up, I proffer out my arm with the robe and towel draped across it. "Take these, you'll need more than the warmth of the fire to get the chill from your bones."

"You are such a fuddy-duddy." She berates me whilst taking my offering. "There's a thrill to the danger, you know? It's what lets you know you're alive."

"If you say so," I wait a moment, biting my lip, before turning around to confirm she's put on the robe. "But do you have to do it in my body?"

This one she doesn't ignore.

"Of course, I do, this poor beautiful thing has been deprived of fun. It needs to be exposed to the gloriousness of nature, of life!" Her arms wave in the air for emphasis, or rather my arms.

"I don't think it does, besides it's my body. Shouldn't I get to decide what it sees and enjoys?"

Again she ignores me, turns her back to me and stares into the fire.

"Isn't it about time you gave it back to me?" My fingers curl and stretch with nervous energy. "The deal was for three days, it's been four. I'm tired of being in this puppet, I want my body back."

"There's still work to be done, I'll need to keep it till that work is complete."

"But you haven't even brought Gillian home, I'm beginning to think you can't." My wooden foot scuffs the floorboards as I twist it back and forth. "I don't really care anymore... I just want to be me again."

She doesn't answer, doesn't even look at me. She might be gone, she could be in the fire right now, and the body in front of me vacant. I can't know for sure, there's no way to really check and even if it is empty, I wouldn't know how to get back in without her help. This was a mistake.

Witches Brew

The brew shifted in the pot, milky tendrils of colour curled outwards from the centre swirling into blemishes of barely distinct browns as they reached the edges. There was a smell akin to burnt toast emanating from the concoction along with something else that she just couldn't place.

"Cinnamon?" She licks her index finger before holding it in the air, trying to discern. "I didn't put in any cinnamon."

Perplexed, she grabs a wooden spoon to give the mixture a stir, the strands of colour vanish blending into the whole. Gently she lifts the spoon up to her nose taking a deep inhale.

"Still cinnamon, now how is that?" Her tongue flicks out for a tiny sample from the spoon, she smacks her lips in quick succession before rubbing her tongue across her teeth. "There definitely isn't any cinnamon in it, perhaps a bit of nutmeg, but there's no cinnamon."

Placing the spoon to one side, hands on her hips she peers into the pot trying to decipher its mystery. The burnt toast smell is becoming stronger, she turns off the heat and glowers at her experiment.

"The recipe doesn't mention a cinnamon smell," She ponders, right hand under her chin with the elbow resting in the palm of her left, "so I must have made an error, but where exactly did I go wrong?"

She paces around the pot and then lets out a heavy sigh, turning her back to it she begins seeking out the recipe book. The answers she seeks must be contained therein.

"Witches brew, witches brew, where in the world is the one for witches brew." She mumbles as she flips through the pages letting out a low whistle, as she finds what she's looking for. "Here it is, now where exactly did we go wrong."

Delicately, using her index finger to draw focus to each line, slowly and intently she reads. As she finishes the first page and her finger lifts at the corner to flip it over, she draws in a deep breath through her teeth.

The page in question is stuck to another, she can feel two separate edges as she runs her finger up and down. This is probably the problem; no, it is most certainly the issue. Gently she prises apart the two pages revealing a sticky stain in the middle of the back page, it completely covers the remaining steps for what she was supposed to do. But her eyes drift to the following page, bulging in their sockets as she reads over the title for the other recipe she intermingled by mistake.

"HOT CHOCOLATE!" She squawks, then quickly covers her mouth. "Hot chocolate?" She whispers as she removes her hand, still staring in puzzlement at the recipe book. "How on earth is it hot chocolate?"

She stares at the page, then looks at the pot, she stares at the page once more and takes in a seething deep breath. Carefully she closes the book just slightly, with her finger between the two previously stuck pages, to look at the cover. *Potent Potions* is written in swooping cursive and just below the title where an author's name should be are the words *love from Mum*. A string of curses escapes from her lips.

Composing herself she opens the book fully and rests it on a counter to avoid the pages re-sticking. With a long exhale she bustles away from the kitchen, out the front door and down the hallway of her apartment building until she comes to a door marked 67. She begins to knock.

"Mother!" She calls in a high pitch just short of what could be described as yelling, "Mother!"

Her mother, an elderly woman with pink hair curlers and a tabby cat slouched over her shoulders, answers the door with bleary eyes and a shushing sound.

"Mother, why does my potions book have a recipe for hot chocolate?" She seethes, trying not to make eye contact with the cat which is staring at her in bewilderment.

"Oh, I thought it might be useful. You always used to enjoy a good mug of hot chocolate." Her mother responds perfectly innocently with a toothy grin. "Wasn't it to your liking? It's the recipe I always used to use for you."

"It is not a matter of if it is to my liking or not, mother. It is a matter of hot chocolate is not a potion and as such should not be in my potions book, and even if it was it certainly shouldn't be right after witches brew."

"Pish posh, it's a beverage. All potions are just fancy beverages with side effects and hot chocolate makes you feel warm and loved so it fits." Her mother absently swats her hand in the air as an act of dismissal.

"But-but-but..." The sentence trails off and she doesn't get the chance to finish her response as her mother slams the door in her face. She stands outside door 67 chastised, upset, and still just a little angry. "That isn't even correct, there are far more criteria for potions. And that doesn't explain putting it right after witches brew." She mumbles to herself as she trudges back to her apartment in defeat. "And I still don't know why mixing the two made it smell like cinnamon."

The smell of burnt toast greets her in a powerful affront as she opens her apartment door, the kitchen is full of wispy smoke despite the fact she turned off the heat. Beating it back with her hands she makes for a window, it takes a bit of hard tugging, but she manages to get it open, the smoke slowly drifts out leaving behind the whiff of cinnamon much to her chagrin.

"Well, we'll mark that one as a failure." A reedy voice emanates from the ceiling, she looks up at it in annoyance.

"It's not exactly my fault the pages were stuck together." She eyeballs the tiny bat clinging to a ceiling hook. "You could have offered some assistance, that's what familiars are supposed to do."

"I was trying not to inhale the fumes." It turns its head away from her gaze, pulling its wings close to form a cocoon around itself. "You'd think the burnt toast smell should have been more concerning than the cinnamon."

"Witches brew is supposed to smell awful, and unique to the witch that's brewed it. Mum's brew smelt like smelly socks, and you never complained about that." She walks away as she speaks, away from the window and the tiny bat and back to her kitchen. "We'll just have to start fresh."

"In that case couldn't you account the cinnamon smell to it being your own unique scent? Perhaps burnt toast and cinnamon is your twist on witches brew."

"That's, well, I... that's preposterous, clearly I messed up the recipe because of the stuck pages and—

"And witches brew can be made any way a witch chooses, maybe mingled with hot chocolate is your take on it. Otherwise, how will you ever be able to know you got it right?"

She bites her tongue trying to come up with some retort to her familiar, yet she's left flummoxed. Indeed, cinnamon and burnt toast weren't so bad and it couldn't really be considered a loss to have a less affronting signature than smelly socks, could it?

My Own Coffin

There were certain eventualities and consequences Emi was willing to admit had slipped her mind when she rose from the dead. She was willing to bet that a lot of things would slip anyone's mind after waking up in a coffin, brain degradation after death and all that had to cause some level of forgetfulness. So, in terms of things, her mistakes had to be viewed as totally reasonable ones to make, right?

Mistake number one was assuming from waking up in the coffin that she was buried already. In her defence, the casket was closed. But she wasn't underground, that had become abundantly clear when the lid had popped open with relative ease.

"OH MY GOD!" Katrina's high-pitched wail was not among the things Emi's mind had forgotten whilst dead.

"Z-z-z-z-ZOMBIE!" Petra and Tegan for all their horror movie consumption, were the first to scramble for the exits when Emi sat up to take in her surroundings. She caught sight of the pair pushing past her elderly grandmother in a mad dash to get outside, she couldn't help but laugh.

That was mistake number two. People who hadn't yet registered her rising from the dead as a horrifying occurrence quickly picked up on that idea when the grating, strained noise departed her lips. It was utter pandemonium as the guests began a mixture of screaming and running in fear, and being morbidly curious about what was happening with her.

"Well, this isn't going well." Emi muttered under her breath. Her voice sounded wrong, it was creepy, she decided to ditch attempting to speak. Later when her brain was less frazzled deductive reasoning would suggest her vocal cords had been injured before death, that, and the decay she was already experiencing had done a nice little number on her voice. For the moment though she was about to head right into mistake three.

Lacking an understanding of her death and frazzled by the on-going panic Emi made the choice to split the funeral parlour. Without stopping to grab a coat or make a trip to the bathroom to inspect her appearance, she headed straight out the window and onto the street. In retrospect she understood this had been a bad plan, she wasn't certain how she'd died but the closed casket at her funeral should have been a hint that something about her appearance might be a bit jarring for people. The shrieks and wails of passers-by in the street jumping away from the sight of her confirmed this information.

Police sirens were the real nail in the proverbial coffin for Emi, the sirens and the lights coming around a corner at speed towards her seemed to cause everything to click together. She'd been dead and her body was noticeably still 'dead'. Given the over-saturation of zombie media, this was an extremely bad situation.

Allowing panic and instinct to take over, Emi turned on her heel running as fast as she could. Given all the talk of slow zombies, Emi was thankful she wasn't too much slower than she'd been in life, but it still wasn't going to be fast enough to escape the police. She made a very logical choice; she went back to the funeral parlour.

Scrambling through the window she'd previously escaped out of, she was a touch surprised to land on a soft surface. Delighted surprise turned to frustration as a lid fell over whatever she'd landed in plunging her into a strangely familiar darkness.

"Oh good, I've climbed into my own coffin." Emi huffed, about to push the lid off for the second time that day, before a moment of consideration. "Oh, good."

Nobody was going to look for the zombie in its coffin, that just didn't happen. With a bit of patience, night would fall and she could make a proper escape.

There were problems with the plan, but as the minutes crawled by Emi considered that they were 'liveable' problems - such as she could still live if she simply endured them. Number one was she had no idea what time it had been when she arose, she knew the sun was out, but that wasn't a lot to go off. It could have been anytime between 10 am and 2 pm, she hadn't exactly had time to check a clock and her family hadn't been so thoughtful as to bury her with a watch.

Problem one led directly to number two, being stuck in a coffin was boring. How was Emi supposed to wait things out if she didn't know how long that would be and had no way to pass said time? On the upside, she quickly grasped that she no longer needed to breathe because otherwise, surely, she'd have passed out from the lack of oxygen inside the coffin.

"I wonder how long I've been dead for?" Speculation Emi decided would have to be how she spent her time, perhaps if she thought over things enough, she could avoid a repeat of her awakening. "Is it summer still? I didn't notice any changes in the leaves or a chill in the air... can I even feel temperatures properly now?"

"How messed up do I look? My casket was closed and those people on the street seemed pretty freaked out. Is my neck messed up? I don't feel like any of my parts aren't in the right spot." With a little squirming she could move her arms around, Emi patted her legs and chest with her hands trying to gauge where the damage was. "I don't really feel anything, but these clothes are a bit thicker than I'd normally wear. First thing when I get out of here, I need to find a mirror and give myself a once over, maybe I can cover it up whatever it is."

Outside the coffin seemed to be quiet. Emi chewed her lips wondering if it'd be a bad idea to sneak a peek. They could be lying in wait for her, or someone could be silently mourning her outside... her body made a weird noise as she found herself inclined to snort derisively.

"Okay, so that's unpleasant." She scrunched her nose in disgust, her voice she supposed she could deal with but this bizarre grotesque alteration to her laughter she was distinctly not a fan of.

"How'd I even come back to life, anyway?" She whispered to herself creaking the coffin lid open to look around, the problem with that was the coffin opened towards the window so she couldn't exactly get a good look at the room by just opening it up a smidge. "Like is one of my friends a necromancer or some shit? Am I the first zombie? Is this like a weird new virus, is that how I died?"

The possibility of danger slipped Emi's mind again as she threw the coffin lid open wide and slipped out for a better look, in the second stroke of luck for her new life there was nobody in the room. Carefully she tip-toed from the parlour to the hallway, the lacking need to breathe made it incredibly easy to move whilst holding her breath to contain any unwanted noises.

Down the hallway, she crept until stumbling upon the sign for the ladies' room. Bathrooms meant mirrors, just what Emi was after. Gingerly she pushed the heavy door open to sneak a peek, nobody was at the sinks and she couldn't hear any noises from the stalls so presumably it was empty. Not wasting a moment, Emi slid into the room heading directly for the mirrors to get a good look at herself.

"Well, that's not great." Makeup wouldn't be enough to cover up the large gaping hole in her cheek, she could just imagine that at some point it'd had skin dangling free over it, they must have neatened it up for her burial. There was also a nasty stitched-up cut along her forehead, but that wasn't so bad. "Now for the rest of it."

Another quick glance around the room to be sure nobody was there and then Emi was throwing off her clothes, she'd been dressed in three layers of tops with leggings and stockings underneath the long ornate skirt she was certain her mother had insisted she be buried in. Underneath was not a pretty sight, there was a kind of faux skin patched over her ribs and she could just make out the bones beneath. Her left leg was not completely her own, it'd been supplemented with a cheap prosthetic joining her thigh to her foot which begged the question "Where the hell is the rest of my leg?"

Sensation, Emi had to presume that along with any sense of temperature, she'd also lost all other forms of sensation because otherwise, she was pretty damn sure she'd have realised that she was walking around on a partial prosthetic. Her arms weren't supplemented by anything but it was hard not to notice now how the right one was dislocated, she couldn't feel it and it didn't seem to wildly affect her ability to move it but for a proper living person it'd be off-putting. There were a few more patch jobs around her chest and stomach.

For a long-drawn-out moment, Emi just stood there in front of the mirror taking in the sight of her body, vastly changed from how she last remembered it. Even her eyes were different, murky and dull, not the vibrant blue they'd been in life. It was strange, disconcerting, and upsetting.

"What happened to me?" Everything, before she woke up, was darkness, or bright and happy memories, she was clearly missing a good chunk of whatever had happened in the lead-up to her death. "I look like wild animals had a go at me... Did wild animals get to my corpse before they found me?"

She mused at the mirror, tracing the damages with her fingers and trying to piece it all together but she could barely feel the touch and without any memory how was she supposed to make sound guesses? It was an exercise in futility she decided, pulling her gaze away from the mirror and searching out her clothes. As she put them back on, she left the skirt behind and only used one of the shirts, her parents were being overly cautious in choosing to dress her in so many layers.

"Okay, the first thing I need to do is find a mask or something to cover this hole." She mumbled to herself as she exited the bathroom, "Second thing, I need a coat or something that's baggy and will hide the dislocation. Or maybe someone who can pop it back, no that's silly it's probably stuck otherwise they'd have fixed it when they prepped me for burial."

From the end of the hallway, Emi could hear voices talking, catching the odd phrase about an escaped stiff was enough for her to piece together it had something to do with her and probably involved at least one police officer. With that information she didn't have many options left for escape, she'd have to find another parlour room or somewhere with a window, she could use as an exit... preferably one that didn't open out onto the street this time. She had to hope that she'd also track down a clock while she was indoors.

The clock was an easy find, an exit path less so. Door one on Emi's search revealed a small kitchenette, the counter covered with trays of biscuits and finger food, this might very well have been food for her wake. A microwave displayed the time from its place above the counter on a small shelf, and the lime-green digital numbers showed 15:57. She'd have a few hours of daylight to kill before dark, if she left now she'd struggle to hide her appearance.

Biting her lip Emi glanced at the clock and then back at the hallway where the sounds of conversation still echoed. If she left now she'd have to stick to the shadows to avoid being spotted, if she's caught there's a strong likelihood of being shot or detained for experimentation. "Would being shot hurt? Can I die again?" Emi mused aloud to herself while staring down the hallway. "Is it a zombie movie thing, like no it won't hurt but if they get me in the head I'll die again? I really wish I had a bit more info on this."

What she would give to have paid attention to Tegan's zombie rants now. The voices suddenly picked up in volume and the distinct shuffle of boots along the carpet served as a prompt for Emi to move. She'd need to decide fast what she was going to do or else this new life of hers wouldn't last long.

"Uhhh..." Panicked she ran out of the kitchenette back down the hallway away from the voices and back to her coffin. "Please don't be coming to check the coffin."

Emi was never good at making spur-of-the-moment decisions in life, coming back to life certainly didn't change that. With haste she scrambled back into her coffin and pulled the lid firmly back down over herself, muttering prayers of hope that they didn't need to check her hiding spot. Surely the coffin should have already been searched. And if not perhaps if she lay perfectly still, they'd just think this was all a big hoax enacted by her former friends in poor taste.

If her heart could still beat Emi's sure it'd be hammering away at her ribs hard enough to break them, if she needed to breathe, she was certain she'd be struggling with holding it, as it was though her main concern was her eyes. She had to think about things seriously, should her eyes be open or closed if and when they opened the coffin? On the one hand, it'd be easier to pretend she's a completely lifeless corpse if they were closed but on the other hand, would it be more normal for her eyes to be open? She wished in that moment she'd been to more funerals before now because it'd certainly help to have some kind of frame of reference.

Eyes scrunched shut, but she hoped by some miracle looking like they were relaxed, Emi took on the appearance of what she was supposed to be; a perfectly normal corpse – not a reanimated zombie. Seconds crept by turning into exhaustingly long minutes, but nothing happened. Outside the coffin she could hear the barest of noises, the silk lining and thick panels of wood served as outstanding noise mufflers when assisted by the fact she was pretty certain her ears were filled with embalming liquid or something.

Nobody opened the coffin, what they did do was move it. Emi held back the urge to make a noise when she felt the coffin's weight shift and sway, the movements made her marginally dizzy but she figured that was a fair trade off for not being discovered. Every now and then there would be an odd stop start or a jolt of the weight being jostled that made Emi concerned it might not be her decision for her corpse to come tumbling out.

There was faint mumbling outside from whoever was doing the carrying, two people Emi assumed at least. It was only after they'd reached wherever it was they were going that she started to be able to make out what they were saying, her ear pressed firmly to the coffin lid.

"So we're just going to store it here?"

"That's right, the Chief wants it kept aside so that when the corpse is recovered she can be properly buried. Family's already been through enough without this whole zombie fiasco, they deserve to be able to bury their daughter properly."

"Aye, fair enough. Let me get a label for it."

It took an unseemly amount of time for the people to leave, Emi could feel nervous energy coiling through her body just itching to get out. When at last she figured she'd waited long enough since the voices had stopped, she pushed hard against the coffin lid expecting it to pop open easily as it had done before. However, it didn't budge. She pushed again, this time using her legs but still it wouldn't give.

Emi repeated her attempts on and off for what felt like days, but the result never changed, she was trapped in her coffin.

"So much for getting to bury me properly, they're never going to find me trapped here in my own coffin. God this is going to be a boring eternity."

Ginger Vampires

"Oh my god, I just freaking love garlic bread!" Josie exclaimed as she went to grab another slice.

"You really do," Cassie wasn't partaking in the extra garlicy, extra cheesy delicacies her friends had put out. No Cassie didn't do garlic breath. Instead, Cassie was sipping tea and munching on crackers like an old Nan.

"Cassie, come on, just one piece. You've gotta try it!" Zane had not learned, every time they were at a party he'd try to get Cassie to try new things and every time he failed.

"No, I really don't."

"Zane, come on, don't worry about Cass. If she doesn't want any that just means more for me, and I'm all good with that." A flirtatious grin played on Josie's face as she looped her arm over Zane's shoulders and winked at Cassie before devouring another piece of carbohydrate goodness.

"But Cass, if you don't have any of the garlic bread how are you gonna keep vampires away?" Dean came out of the kitchen with two more platters of garlic bread.

"Vampires don't exist, Dean, that's how I'm going to keep them away. So excuse me while I pass on the bad breath." Cassie took another long sip of her tea.

The party continued on into the late hours of the night and as the wee hours of the morning began so too did an erratic screeching noise.

"What the hell is that sound?" Josie tried to cover her ears but still, the noise would not cease.

"It's probably racoons, Dean let's go check it out." Ever the hero, getting up from the couch, Zane grabbed a flashlight.

"Or maybe it's Vampires! Good thing we ate all that garlic bread." Dean quickly followed Zane, whilst Cassie rolled her eyes at them.

"Yeah, whatever. Don't hurt yourselves." She got up too but not to go investigate the noise, "I'll be here drinking some more of your tea."

The boys went out to investigate and slowly time ticked by.

"It's been like twenty minutes, and that weird noise is still persisting. Should we go check on them?" Josie was standing in front of the windows, staring into the night when Cassie looked up from her teacup.

"I guess, like it's no big deal. They're probably just hanging about trying to prank us, but if you wanna check it out Josie then we will." Slowly Cassie pulls herself up from the lounge, joining Josie in front of the windows.

"*Gulp* Yeah, let's uh, let's check it out." Josie grasped her hand. Josie's hand was covered in sweat but still, Cassie gave it a squeeze.

"It'll be fine Josie, there's nothing out here that could hurt us."

With that said the girls ventured out into the night, in search of the boys. As they wandered into the garden the screeching got louder, until it was almost deafening. There was no sign of the boys anywhere, and Cassie could feel Josie trembling... she could also feel eyes watching them.

"Guys, come out already. I know you're there. Come on, let's go back inside. Guys?" Cassie called out into the darkness but there was no response. There was a rustling in the bushes, but the girls couldn't make out any noises over the deafening sound of the screeching.

A tall, shadowy figure emerged from the bushes, creeping up behind the girls who stood in place.

"Guys? Zane! Dean!" Cassie was calling out at the top of her lungs hoping for a response. Behind them the shadowy figure crept up to Josie and in a quick motion bit into her neck, covering her mouth with its hand. Through this, Cassie kept calling for the boys until she felt Josie's hand go limp.

Pivoting to look at Josie her blood ran cold. She wanted to scream but the words caught in her throat, it was as if her whole body was petrified. Frozen in fear she watched the ghastly creature sucking the life from her friend. Small strands of blood dribbling from its lips, cascading down the pale flesh of Josie's neck. Slipping her hand from Josie's, and moving backwards, her heart sank as she bumped against something.

Cassie would have fainted but was too petrified to even do that. She could feel breathing upon her neck, and a cold claw-like hand resting on her shoulder. Her flesh felt like it would break out in goosebumps. Each second ticking past seemed like an eternity. The breathing was intensifying, getting closer, a mouth moving towards her neck terrifying her. Then it happened, lips closing down upon her skin. Preparing for pain and death she winced at the cool touch, yet nothing happened.

There was no piercing of her skin, just a sucking noise before the lips peeled off her and another hand came to rest on her other shoulder. Spinning her around to face the something. Cassie's heart dropped, it was Zane but his face was twisted and wrong. He smiled at her.

"You really didn't touch any of the garlic bread, tsk, tsk Cassie. And ginger tea, why Cass aren't you smart." He caressed her cheek and then her neck.

"W-what are you?" Cassie managed to squeeze out the words, her skin trembling under his cold touch.

"Why I'm a Vampire of course." He grinned, displaying all his teeth, unlike the grins he had shown her before this one was full of sharp spikes.

"B-b-but vampires hate garlic, and, and you ate like four pieces of the garlic bread. Josie ate the garlic bread." Zane chuckled as she squeaked out the words.

"Yeah about that, you see it's a common misconception that we vamps dislike garlic. What we really don't like is *ginger*." Putting a finger to her lips, he made a shushing sound so she wouldn't protest, "Garlic actually helps us. It's yummy and lets us walk in the sunlight. But ginger, ginger is a no-go; it tastes yuck and burns our throats. I can smell it all over you, I could smell it in your tea, and it was so strong I nearly gagged. That's why I wanted you to eat some garlic bread, make you nice and tasty." His finger ran over her bottom lip.

"I-is Dean a vampire too?" Panicking, Cassie couldn't help but think what would be next for her if they couldn't eat her. What would they do? What hope did she have?

"Nah, Dean's just a... sorry *was* just a frat boy. He was kind of my middleman, he held parties and I picked off partygoers. It helped that he was always keen to serve the food I made chock full of garlic."

"T-then w-who ate Josie?"

"Aw, that's right - you and Josie were close. Sorry, but you shouldn't have come out here. If you'd stayed inside you would have been fine. Dave over there ate Josie, you've never met him." She wanted to turn and look at Dave, to see Josie's killer with her own eyes, but she didn't dare move her gaze from Zane.

"How would we have been any safer inside? You were inside with us all night." She had to think of some way to escape.

"Don't you know Cassie? We just killed the party host, our invite has been rescinded, I can't go back inside... plus it reeks of ginger from all your tea brewing." *That's it!* A light-bulb went off in Cassie's brain.

"Well, why don't you take a whiff of this!" Blowing air into Zane's face made him cringe and back away. Not wasting a second Cassie ran for the house. She was almost in range of the glass doors when suddenly she lost her footing. Before she could get up Zane was upon her.

"Naughty girl, Cassie. I can't have you getting away now you know the truth. No, I've got something special planned for you." Zane flashed her that wicked grin and punched her; everything went dark.

Cassie's eyes strained against the sunlight, her head hurting.

"I must've had too much to drink last night..." Cassie trailed off remembering the timid night of tea and crackers while her friends boozed it up and gobbled garlic bread. "Josie, let's go home," she calls out, before realising she wasn't in the house... although she was in a house.

"Josie?" Nothing looks familiar, and it seems she's in a bedroom... although why was she asleep on the floor then?

"Oh, you're up?" A voice came from behind her; Cassie spun around to see Zane - shirtless and in a set of track pants.

Was this his place? Why would she be here instead of at Dean's?

"Uh, yeah. How'd I end up here?" Cassie's brain felt hazy, she couldn't seem to remember anything from last night.

"Oh, you know, we spent the night together. You gave me a lift and crashed here."

"That... doesn't sound right, I mean if anyone was going to hook up with you last night it would have been Josie... and if I was going to hook up with anyone it would have been with Josie too." This all seemed weird, Cassie knew somehow that what Zane was saying was wrong.

"Oh yeah? Then how come you've got a hickey from me on your neck?" Cassie felt her neck, she couldn't feel anything different. Chuckling, Zane pulled out his phone.

"Look here." In the reflective surface, she can see a red mark on her neck.

"It just doesn't seem like that's what happened." Cassie replied, pushing the phone away.

"Well, maybe a little breakfast will make things clearer?" Zane placed a hand on her back steering her towards the door.

"I guess, I could go for breakfast."

"Good, I made something special."

They reached the kitchen, on the bench-top sat a beautiful omelette, Cassie's stomach growled. She dug into the food with little concern. "Mmm, this is really good."

"Yeah?"

"Sooo, good. But there's a little bit of an odd flavour to it?"

"Oh, that'd be the garlic." Zane grinned as she stuffed another bite into her mouth.

A Touch of Fantasy

Season of Blood

The violins grate on Tiffany's ears as she descends the stairs into the ballroom, the light from the chandeliers is practically blinding so she keeps her eyes downturned, her lips form a closed smile to hide her clenched teeth. A lady does not ball her fists so Tiffany waves with her free hand while her other strokes the railing, every few seconds her occupied fingers bend just slightly in want to grip the rail but she holds firm. Everything must appear perfect; her mask cannot fall for even a second.

Eager suitors meet her at the bottom of the staircase, practically stumbling over themselves to see who can offer her their arm first as they all clamour for the chance of a dance. She breaths in deeply through her nose, exhaling slightly and fixing her smile before opening her mouth.

"Sir Thompson I'd be delighted to dance with you." She accepts a nobleman's arm, feigning compassion with her eyes for those she is in effect turning down.

Her fangs hurt dreadfully from being rescinded as she converses politely with her dance partner, but it is a pain she has to endure and far less than that she'd previously endured when on her monthlies. This ball has been months in the planning, her benefactor insisted it was a necessary celebration alongside being a compulsory test of her restraint; one she would need to pass with exceedingly good results if she wished to continue down the path her benefactor had opened up to her. So yes, she will endure the pain—any pain.

Aromas are rich in the air. A collection of varied perfumes and colognes, they tickle her nose in its newfound sensitivity, but she says a quiet prayer of thanks that amongst all the smells there isn't even the faintest whiff of blood. It is no mean feat to avoid the lure of the metallic scent; she finds it near impossible, but it is necessary to keep her composure.

"I was concerned by your absence last season, there was talk you'd fallen dreadfully ill." Sir Thompson's remark as they dance causes a slight tremor of discontent beneath her skin, but Tiffany gives nothing away, instead, she opts to bat her eyelashes and mollify him with a smile.

"Alas my health was not ideal for travel last season," She picks her words with care, speaking with a honeyed tone, "Thankfully, God has graced me with perfect health this season."

"I am gladdened to hear that." That's done the trick, Sir Thompson moves their conversation on from the unwelcome discussion to simpler things.

She partakes in five dances altogether before taking a break, two with Sir Thompson, two with a couple of different gentlemen whose names she's already forgotten, and a final dance with her benefactor. They did not talk during their dance, but Tiffany knows he was appraising her, looking for any signs that her mask was slipping.

It is when she takes to the balcony for fresh air after dancing that her benefactor speaks to her. She'd not noticed him following her, even when he stands beside her, she's barely able to grasp his presence. There is clearly much more that she will need to learn if she passes tonight.

"You should dance with Sir Thompson when you return inside, it would be good for you if he was to make a proposal." Her benefactor, Doctor Greeves, leans on the balcony railing as he lights up a pipe.

"Would it?" Tiffany's hands fidget at her sides, resisting the urge to hold her cheeks for the pain in her mouth. "I will not be able to bear children as I am, that would surely rouse suspicion."

"It will rouse more suspicion if you do not wed, spinsters are keenly watched." He draws in a deep breath before exhaling a plume of smoke through the pipe. "Besides, as your doctor, I can remedy the lack of a pregnancy and a child. There are plenty of babies that go orphaned, it is no trouble to collect one and present it as if it were your own."

"You don't think he'd notice that I never have the monthlies?" She spares a glance back into the hall, exceedingly aware she cannot spare much more time away from the proceedings inside lest she incite rumour.

"Doubtful, I know very few men who take notice of such a thing. And if you let him bed you often enough, he is sure to never wonder about it." It's not a suggestion, Tiffany grasps it then. This is the criteria for her passing, she must attain a husband.

"Very well, if that is what it takes." She allows herself a moment of ire, and then she recovers completely, turning to go back inside.

"It is if you want me to continue as your benefactor." Doctor Greeves' words are in a whisper, but she knows the weight with which they are said, "You know what the alternative is."

The alternative is unacceptable, that is what Tiffany knows because the alternative is a most painful and excruciating death.

"I know." She whispers more to herself than the doctor as she returns to the ballroom in search of Sir Thompson.

It's easier than she expected to secure the man's proposal, but she doesn't spare a moment for suspicion after all it's something she too is urgently in need of. With her benefactor's support, they marry before the season is even over.

Their marriage bed is large, ornate, and frankly a little gaudy in Tiffany's opinion. Sir Thompson is a man of great wealth, but his home is run by a minute amount of staff; both of his parents passed from this world and with his military service behind him Tiffany expected a slight bit more luxury and taste within the estate. There will be time to make changes to all of that of course after they've consummated their marriage.

She waits for her husband, bearing the pain of her teeth all the while as she keeps them concealed. Just a little while longer, when the consummation is done, she will seek out a feed. Her benefactor provided her sustenance before the wedding ceremony but as another test, he'd informed her strictly that she was not to feed from then until after the act of consummation. Now her hunger pangs feel near impossible, but she needs to resist them; drinking from her husband is most definitely not permissible.

When the floorboards outside creak and the door to their chambers begins to squeak open, Tiffany breathes a sigh of relief. Soon the waiting will be over. Relief, however, turns to a lump in her throat as the thick, heady smell of blood greets her nostrils. It is tantalising and almost irresistibly intoxicating, she bites her lip to muffle a whimper of desire as her husband enters the room.

The sight that greets her is unexpected, she pierces her lip with the bite of her fangs and a squeal of shocked delight. Sir Thompson enters the room but is hardly alone, draped over his shoulders is a pale-looking woman and just behind him Doctor Greeves smiling with far too many teeth. Red stains speckle her husband's white nightshirt and there's the slightest speckle of blood still clinging to his jaw.

It would hardly take a genius to appraise the situation at hand, and in the moment of piecing it all together, Tiffany licks her lips with curious desire.

"Congratulations are in order, you've both passed with flying colours." Doctor Greeves declares as Sir Thompson throws the pale woman onto the bed, "Enjoy your feed and consummation. During the break, we'll organise a child for you both and move on with your training, in a few seasons' time the two of you may even be up to working as benefactors."

"Do you think so?" Sir Thompson asks whilst removing his shirt, his question for the Doctor although his eyes linger on Tiffany.

"I don't see why not, you're the first pair that have successfully found each other in thirty years. You'll work well for moving our society forward." The Doctor sucks his fangs back in, clearing his throat. "Provided you manage to go unsuspected."

"Then—" Tiffany wipes a thread of drool from her mouth, looking up from the bleeding woman to ask the Doctor a question but he hushes her.

"Enough, the rest of the night is for the two of you. We will talk again in the morning. Goodnight, Sir and Lady Thompson."

When the Doctor leaves the couple do not speak, the intoxicating scent of blood enthrals them until the woman on their bed is drained completely of the substance. They push her corpse to the ground as they finish feeding before moving on to the other activity they were instructed to perform by their benefactor.

--

The season has started again, Tiffany bounces her *son* upon her hip as she stares down from the banister to the ballroom below. Her keen eyes easily trace her husband making the rounds greeting guests, and the subtle hand signals he makes for her private acknowledgment assessing the candidates for feeding and those for turning. Doctor Greeves is present too, a new young lady clinging to his arm clearly nervous for her first foray into polite society. It's a cruel pick, Tiffany thinks, there's little chance the girl from a previously impoverished background will manage to pass the tests of their society.

"Ma. Ma. Ma" Coos Patrick from her hip, crying for her attention.

"Yes, yes, little one." She lifts him to her face and nuzzles her nose to his. "You will fare much better when it's your turn."

"He will." Her husband surprises her with a whisper against the ear. He's progressing with lessons much faster than her, Tiffany's brow creases at that thought, then diffuses with a smile as she turns to face him.

"Dorian, you're supposed to be with the guests." She giggles as her husband brushes a kiss against her cheek.

"I know, I know, and I'll be right back to my duties after I give Patrick a cuddle." He gestures for her to pass their *son* to him.

"Very well, but just a quick cuddle. You'll be able to have plenty of them when we switch places later for my feeding break." The mere thought of the feed to come makes Tiffany salivate, she smacks her lips and licks her tongue across her teeth to stave off the thought.

"Careful love, your fangs are showing. We don't want to scare Patrick." He passes the boy back to her, pressing a kiss to his forehead before brushing one to the back of her hands. "I will see you both again soon."

"Pick me out a nice one," She calls after him as he descends the stairs.

Patrick copies her by burbling out nonsense sounds and waving his arms. The baby boy has no inkling that they are not his parents by blood or that they are far from ordinary people, he's grown pleasantly attached. It's a good thing, Tiffany thinks, it keeps her and Dorian from wanting to feed on the sweet thing.

"Sir Dorian Thompson, just the man I wanted to see." Down below she can hear people cloying for her husband's attention, mostly businessmen after an investment but there is the odd young woman in the mix hoping to catch his eye.

Tiffany licks her lips, perhaps one of those girls will be her feed for the night. There's something indescribably satisfying about draining a woman who seeks to seduce her husband, a young woman from a background not so different to her own with a proper upbringing is a taste so much more refined than their normal fare.

"You're drooling."

"And you're lurking," Tiffany wipes her free hand across her mouth, "you shouldn't be up here, doctor."

"I know." Her benefactor states coming to stand beside her at the banister. "But I thought it good form to greet both my hosts tonight and to check on sweet Patrick."

"Most gracious of you." Tiffany sighs, it's never easy making conversation with Doctor Greeves. "What about your prospect? She was clinging to you last I saw, where is she now?"

"On the dance floor with a young gentleman."

"She won't make the cut, you know." Tiffany searches out the girl with her eyes, absentmindedly bouncing Patrick on her hip.

"We'll see, the season is only just starting she may well manage."

That was true. And what a season it would be; her first season of blood.

Witches Hollow

The students of Witchbane Academy were astir, High Sorceress Melisandre Wolsmitt was coming. Freshman dormitories had been abuzz with rumours about the famed Witch of Wonders, senior dormitories giddy with nerves over the Enchantments Competition she would be hosting and everyone was after a glimpse of her ride.

"It's said that she rides a fiery Chimera!"

"Poppycock, you can't ride a Chimera. *She* rides a splendid liquorice Pegasus!"

"That's all hogwash, she doesn't ride a creature. Everybody knows she drives a classic Austin-Healey."

Everyone had heard a different story and they all thought they were right. As it turned out, she arrived in a multi-coloured tendril of smoke.

Melisandre Wolsmitt was herself astir, she wanted to drink in everything that had changed at her Alma Mater. Not to mention her delight at being able to show off her brand new, bouncing baby boy to all her old friends who were now professors.

Once the students caught sight of the baby all disappointment at not being right vanished and now they all simply needed to get a closer look at the adorable little warlock.

She'd named him Charon after her favourite Greek God, he was an absolute sweetheart who barely ever fussed. Any student who successfully mastered their nerves to come to speak to her was greeted with Melisandre's signature toothy grin and a conspiratorial look. "Do you want to see my little boy?"

"Oh yes!"

Everyone was enamoured with him. It was a small comfort that Melisandre took to heart when it was finally time to leave after her lecture. She bounced Charon on her hip, conjuring up her travelling smoke as she quietly contemplated the future. It's a shame she thinks, all these young witches who adore the sight of him now will barely spare Charon a glance when he's older. They'll be disappointed he doesn't have the spark to be a great warlock. He'll only ever be able to use simple magic.

Charon cooed at her as they vanished from the academy grounds, and giggled happily when they reappeared at home. He might not have the spark but there was a fire to his eyes.

"Aren't you just the most handsome warlock." Melisandre smiled at her baby, bringing him up to her face for a kiss. "It doesn't matter how powerful you become; Mother will always love you."

--

This was the day she had been waiting for, she could feel the excitement bubbling over inside as she stood stock still looking at the gates.

Witchbane Academy the foremost institute for gramarye, lorded as the most prestigious school in twelve realms, and the main attraction of Witches Hollow. She could hardly believe she was here, she'd been accepted for study, all those gods' forsaken days of painstakingly studying for exams had paid off in the end. A wicked grin snaked its way onto her face, this was going to be fun.

All she needed to do was waltz up to the gates and brandish her letter of acceptance for them to swing right open. Left foot first she crossed onto the campus' sacred grounds. For the first time in her life, Danica Molwif was in awe, the shimmering splendour of enchantment was all over the buildings and there was a pungent smell wafting over the quad which could only be a hex brew.

"Finally, I'm here." Danica whispered to herself as she set off in search of the dorm, which would be her home for the next few years. When she left, she'd be one of the greatest masters of gramarye there ever was.

But first, she would have to learn the arts, and perhaps, begrudgingly, make friends.

--

"Welcome to your first official potions class ladies, my name is Professor Aria Salmanda. I'll be instructing you today and for the rest of your hapless days here at Witchbane Academy on the art of concocting." Professor Aria Salmanda was intimidating, tall and strikingly beautiful, and there was no doubt this was a powerful witch.

Every one of the first years held their breath as the professor strode through the room passing out recipes for their first potions assessment. Danica was in awe of the power and respect the Professor commanded, that's what she wanted, power. Of course, she understood to reach such a goal she'd first need to pass her assessment, so she ceased looking at the Professor after receiving her recipe.

Scanning the ingredients list, Danica softly repeated the words under her breath.

"Eye of newt, Toad's breath, pickled tongue, cackleberry, speckled toadstool and vulture claw..." she paused after reading the list, backtracking through the ingredients. "Cackleberry? What's that?" she mused aloud, but at a whisper so as not to let Professor Salmanda know she was ignorant of what must surely be a common potions ingredient.

"It's an egg," whispered one of the girls at the workstation across from her. Danica fixed the girl with a stare, she was furious that somebody had heard her and that she was being corrected but she had to contain that anger, what mattered was passing the assessment. She took in a deep breath.

"What type of egg?" Danica hissed, she wasn't happy that she needed to ask, but she'd be damned if she let her pride ruin everything when she'd only just started.

"An egg, you know from a hen." The girl, who was short and a little on the big side, must have thought Danica was daft for asking what kind of egg, but in witchcraft, you could never be too careful with these things.

Instead of responding with a vicious retort Danica nodded and turned her back to the girl. There were a dozen things she'd like to say but there wasn't time for that, and while she had no intentions of becoming friends with anyone at the academy, least of all somebody who knew one of her shortcomings, she also didn't precisely want to make enemies just yet.

Bristling with quiet rage Danica went to the ingredients cabinet and gathered what she needed, in proper school fashion nothing was labelled, and it was yet another test for students to prove they knew what they were doing.

Back at her workstation Danica set-up her cauldron and followed the recipe:

1. Wash the speckled toadstool then put it into the cauldron before filling with cold water.
2. Bring water to a boil and add pickled tongue, vulture claw and eye of newt.
3. Keep the pot at a simmer and stir for 5 minutes before cracking open the cackleberry and putting the yolk into the mixture.
4. Add Toad's breath and put a lid onto the pot to keep it from escaping, turn off the flame and leave the cauldron to sit for an hour.

When she returned to the cauldron Danica was surprised at how sweet the potion smelled, she checked the recipe but there were no more steps or notes. She looked for a name to the potion, but the Professor had left it blank leaving the students to discover for themselves what they had made. That's when a wicked idea came to mind, Danica took a spoon and ladled out some of the mixture into a bowl then took it over to the girl who'd helped her before.

"Hi, I'm Danica, thanks for your assistance earlier."

"Oh no problem, we're all here to learn the craft after all. I'm Nerin." The girl smiled sweetly and shook Danica's hand.

"Would you like some of the potion I made, it's really tasty. Honestly, I think it's just a simple cake recipe I was given, all the ingredients were completely normal."

"Wouldn't surprise me, very few potions I know of require cackleberry. Sure, I'd love a taste." Unsuspectingly the girl took a spoonful of the potion and swallowed it. "It's a little bitter, but otherwise f-" the girl stopped midway and started to give Danica a rather unsettling look, that of a lovesick puppy.

"So, it's a love potion, great." Danica noted the effect and excused herself from Nerin, growing uncomfortable with the girl's stare.

When the Professor returned Danica was happy to find out she was correct and awarded full marks for her assessment. Though Professor Salmanda gave her a bit of a look after noticing Nerin's new behaviour. Not a completely disapproving look, Danica decided seeing as the Professor made no attempt to scold her or to provide an antidote for Nerin's condition.

That simple love potion would become a staple of Danica's, she kept the original recipe sheet for years to come until well after graduation. And well, it never did seem to wear off.

--

"What is that?"

After a long day of classes, Danica had not expected a creature to be in her room. She was certainly not expecting a feather moulter to be perched on her bedhead.

"Sellie, what is this thing?" She turned peevishly to ask her roommate.

It bobbed its head at her. As if it understood that she was talking about it.

"It's a boobook!"

Sellie answered as if Danica should understand, without even bothering to look up from her studies.

"What the hell is a boobook?"

The thing ruffled its wings, cocked its head, and stared at Danica. It was unnerving.

"Well as you can see, it is a small owl. A reddish-brown spotted owl."

Yes, yes, Danica could see that. Still, why was it here? Sellie didn't have a familiar, she was supposed to specialise in animation- she didn't do real creatures. In fact, Danica had specifically requested a roommate without a familiar when she'd applied for housing. If Sellie had suddenly decided to get a familiar now in their second year, well then Danica was going to have to petition for a change in roommates.

"What's it doing here?"

"I made it."

What? What? What?

Danica's head was throbbing. She couldn't quite grasp the situation so she asked again.

"What?"

"It's a golem. I crafted it with clay and brought it to life."

She created it? Danica had never seen Sellie's magic at work, she'd seen golems but nothing this real. It was astonishing and honestly very frustrating... and if it was a golem then it wasn't really a familiar, so it wouldn't be grounds for switching roommates.

"Really?"

Danica had strong magic, but she had never been able to create a golem, let alone something this real. Sellie on the other hand, had always seemed weak, she was terrible at potions and struggled at mastering incantations. So why was it that Sellie could create such a realistic creature and bring it to life, while Danica could not?

"Yes, really. Don't worry it'll be gone tomorrow, I made it for an assignment so I'll be handing it in."

"Oh, good then." Danica rolled her eyes, shooing the boobook from her bed. It was unsettling and it certainly changed Danica's perspective on Sellie but she wouldn't let that bother her. It didn't matter how good her golems were, Danica was still the superior witch... she'd just have to find a way to remind Sellie and herself of that fact.

--

"Do you think spells can account for metathesis?"

"What?" Danica had been chewing her pencil, bored out of her mind until Eliza piped up.

"Perhaps, what do you think Danica?" Nerin chimed, leaning across the desk to bat her doe eyes at her.

"I don't know, why don't you do a thesis on it or something? I'm trying to think of the perfect graduation project." How she had ever come to be surrounded by these two particularly annoying girls she would never comprehend.

"I think I will, it could be interesting. There'll need to be a lot of trials though, do you think I could ask Professor Salmanda to sponsor me for it? There's going to be a lot of risks involved." Eliza, it seemed would not be deterred by Danica's lack of interest, as she continued to drone on. That at least was less frustrating than Nerin's silent pining over Danica.

"Why don't you go ask her now? Isn't it her office hours at the moment." Nerin wasn't planning to just sit and be quiet it seemed, and Danica realised woefully the deluded girl would now be her sole company as Eliza hurried to gather her things.

"Oh, you're right. I'll have to go see her right this minute, I'd hate for someone else to steal my thesis idea pertaining to metathesis!" Eliza whirled out of the room like a hurricane, Danica had never seen the bookish girl move so fast.

"Looks like we're alone, now." Nerin cooed in that lovesick voice she only made when it was just her and Danica. It was astonishing the love potion had never worn off, but Danica was beginning to find the girl's advances more than a little unwelcome.

"Yes, well, perhaps now would be the perfect time for me to go work on a little independent potions study." Danica had to excuse herself to extricate herself from this situation and perhaps finally brew a cure for poor Nerin. "You best finish up your studies though, no need to accompany me."

She was halfway through collecting the necessary ingredients for a cure when another more delicious idea came to mind. A perfect solution to an issue she'd been having with her roommate and one that could double as a graduation project. It'd mean putting off making a cure for Nerin, but Danica decidedly could deal with the lovesick puppy for at least a little longer and she was somewhat curious as to if the original potion's effects would ever wear off.

"Yes, that's perfect. Two birds, one stone." It was decided, Nerin could wait. Crushing Sellie's spirit by stealing her mortal boyfriend and nailing an absolutely perfect graduation project, could not.

--

Sellie was not prepared, not prepared at all. She had left the house in a hurry because she had been late, and you certainly did not want to be late for meeting the one and only High Sorceress Melisandre Wolsmitt. Being late after all would create a bad first impression.

Of all the things that had occurred in her life there was seldom much that Sellie felt uncertain about. She had been uncertain about befriending her roommate in college, which had turned out to be something she most certainly shouldn't have bothered about because Danica had never had the slightest want to be friends. The girl had in fact been so cruel as to use the mortal Sellie had been seeing at the time as a part of her graduation project, in a scheme Sellie was certain had been concocted almost entirely to upset her personally.

Uncertainty had also plagued her about starting up her own business, but that had worked out quite well and she was now the foremost supplier of Golems to all of Witches Hollow. And lastly, she'd been uncertain about going on a date with her handyman, but Charon as it turned out whilst not a strong warlock was the son of none other than Melisandre Wolsmitt.

And now, now she was uncertain about meeting his mother. "What if she doesn't like me?" Sellie kept thinking to herself, "She's the High Sorceress, she's not going to be impressed by my simple magic." And then rather than focusing on the fact she was the High Sorceress, Sellie began focusing on the fact that she was Charon's mother.

"Oh, what if she really doesn't like me? What if she makes him stop seeing me? What if I ruin everything and Charon never talks to me again?"

Her mind was plagued with such thoughts as she reached the restaurant, on time but with no concealer spells on and in a dress that was slightly wrinkled as she hadn't had time to iron it. She went inside, the restaurant was packed. Panicking internally, she looked around nervously till she spotted Charon waving her over.

"Maybe we should have rescheduled, I'm not prepared for this at all." she whispered to herself.

"Relax, Sellie. Mother will love you." Charon softly kissed her cheek and took her hand as she sat down beside him; suddenly all that uncertainty was gone.

--

Sellie loved to garden, ever since she'd gotten a place of her own after graduating from the academy, she'd endeavoured to cultivate the most beautiful garden in Witches Hollow. Before entering her home and place of business, people would be greeted by an array of singing cinquefoils, it was a beautiful sight.

Danica on the other hand had nothing but contempt for gardening, she'd tried her hand at growing her own herbs but found it futile. So, when she arrived at Sellie Judicar's house, she wasn't awed by the garden's beauty or the delicate singing but rather infuriated. She had to hold herself back from burning the entire floral array.

Whatever it was her old roommate had summoned her for must certainly be pressing, considering they hadn't parted on good terms at graduation. And it would be overly wicked, to start off their reunion by burning Sellie's garden. However, Danica made a note to herself that if the meeting wasn't to her liking she could perhaps singe a few of the cinquefoils on her way out.

Making her way up the garden path, Danica found her progress blocked by a large man in the doorway.

"Urgh, get out of the way you big galoot, you lummox, you big dolt!"

He blinks at her. His big soft, fiery eyes flickering open and close. For a moment she is mesmerised by the faint glint in his eyes, and then he moves.

"Sorry."

He mumbles. The barely audible word seems out of place. She finds his soft-spoken manner to conflict with the large, bulky exterior her eyes beheld.

"Ahh, Danica you are here."

A woman appears at the edge of her vision. Slowly, swathed in soft fabrics the woman glides into the frame. Her hand falls on the chest of the galoot.

"I see you've already made the acquaintance of my dear Charon. Isn't he charming?"

Danica's eyes roam over the galoot. He shuffles a little under her gaze, and she smirks, perhaps he had some value- she supposed he was good-looking.

"Well, he's no Greek God."

There's a chuckle from the woman. Charon seems to blush a little and turns just so towards the woman. He mumbles softly into her ear, and her eyebrows cross.

"All right, well I'll see you at dinner then."

She kisses his cheek softly. Her hand caresses his face, and she whispers something into his ear. He leaves, though his eyes linger on the woman for a few moments.

"Yes, Charon is no Greek God, but he's very good to me."

"Is he a Golem then?"

Danica can't help but poke fun. Sellie had never been good with men. However, her speciality was in animation.

"No. He's not a Golem, Danica!"

The words are spat at her fiercely. It's like acid. She always was touchy.

"Please, relax Sellie. He's very large... a bit of a galoot by the looks."

Sellie frowns at her.

"He's not a galoot. I love him and I won't have you nosing about and being mean. Or have you trying to steal him."

Ouch. Sellie has always been intuitive; Danica must admit she's tempted to lure the galoot away- to crush Sellie completely. She'd done it before, hadn't she? It's Sellie's fault if she chooses to trust her again.

"Anyway, I summoned you here to help with something. Shall we?"

Her arm is extended to Danica. It's not lost on Danica how much this must pain Sellie, to ask for her help.

"I suppose." Danica sighs, taking Sellie's arm.

"It's to do with a request from my soon-to-be mother-in-law, and our Alma Mater. Unfortunately, I won't be able to handle it on my own."

Just as the stories foretold

It was all rather unnerving, nobody likes knowing their fate especially not when they are without a doubt certain that the fate they have been told cannot be correct.

"Look again seer, that can't be right." Protested the young Princess Amariy, "It just can't."

"Fine, I will look once more." The seer was a patient woman who had learnt long ago that nobody is willing to just accept their fate. She focused her gaze upon her crystal ball and raised her hands above the revealing tome. "Show me the fate of Princess Amariy of Meliantha, writ into page must her future be, a great and daring story for all to read."

The revealing tome glowed as images flickered through the crystal ball, it was all rather enchanting. And then at last all was still and the seer turned her gaze to the princess. "It is done, read the tome and the stories will foretell your fate."

Princess Amariy snatched up the tome and began to read:

Upon the princess' eighteenth name day, her path will become intertwined with another's, announced it will be and they shall wed. A kingdom of thorns and lies shall she bed as her heart strays from whom it is wed, dark tales and foul deeds not to be said adultery the least of crimes that can be said.

A silver tongue queen shall she be when her love turns to ash in her mouth a bitter pill to swallow. For her heart torn asunder shall the blame fall on the one she called lover a demon in disguise. And so shall it be for her sin all hell shall arise.

"It's exactly the same as it was before, this cannot be right I shall not accept it!" Screamed the Princess throwing the tome out the tower window and storming off, leaving the seer behind.

--

A few years later Princess Amariy celebrated her name day and betrothal to Prince Mallen of Theivor, she wasn't particularly interested in Mallen though- it was simply an arranged marriage. She was much more interested in Mallen's sister Beatrice whose sultry smiles and soft touches left her body tingling.

As their marriage went forth and she moved from Meliantha to the thorny kingdom of Theivor, Amariy found herself even more attracted to Beatrice and it was not long before she found herself in a sultry tryst with her new sister-in-law. Beatrice would whisper many sweet nothings to Amariy and soon Amariy found she would do almost anything for Beatrice, anything.

It was only a few years after her marriage to Mallen that the King of Theivor died, assassinated by Amariy though no one would ever know. And so, it was she became Queen Amariy of Theivor, a queen who excelled with lies. Especially lies about death, yes she would master those after Beatrice told her to kill Mallen, it was a necessity.

Then on the third anniversary of Mallen's death it occurred, Beatrice refused her lover Amariy and laughed, cackled, and the world shook as the earth split apart and demons arose. And then with an ash taste in her mouth, Amariy knew fate was always just as the stories foretold.

Only Luck

The clock was ticking. Tick. Tick. Tick. Stacy could practically feel the movements of the hand as each second passed her by. There wasn't much time. There was never very much time when it came to stopping a murder.

It had taken months for Stacy to master movement over her incorporeal form, weeks to learn how to read auras, days to adjust to the absence of the need to sleep or eat, and years to gain what small amount of impact she could hold on the physical plane of existence. She wasn't about to miss her chance to do some good.

Murder was a horrible way to go. In Stacy's expert opinion, it was the worst way to die. You could deal with death by accident, were generally prepared for dying if an illness took you out, and content if your time was quite literally up because you'd lived it all. But if you were murdered, there was no coping with that. It kept you stuck and denied you the ability to move on to whatever was waiting after life. At least that was Stacy's working theory, she couldn't say for sure that there was no chance of moving on... perhaps if her killer was brought to justice and she managed to feel somehow complete in how she'd lived her life maybe then she could move on.

She didn't really have time to contemplate all of that though, not right this minute, not when she could be stopping somebody else from sharing her fate. The trick was she'd have to time it exactly, and then it'd be up to the victim to generate a bit of luck. Five times out of ten luck would be enough. The other times, Stacy didn't like to dwell on.

The girl; dressed to the nines in a sleek velvet dress with diamonds dripping from her hair, ears, and neck, was cornered. It was a side street, with just one precise turn which was hidden from the streetlights, a perfect spot for those who wanted to be hidden for a moment and planned to escape by blending in with the general populace.

Her attacker looked like a thug from an old-timey detective movie, what with their long tan trench coat and a broad-brimmed hat. They were quiet, and discreet, with no intention of giving away their identity; not to the girl, not to anyone else they would pass in the street.

Whatever method of attack they planned; the darkness would hide the girl from knowing until it was too late. But that wasn't an issue for Stacy, ghosts don't need lights to see; everything since her death existed in a soft haze of colour with auras working as flashes of vibrancy lighting up the world. It would be a knife, she could make it out barely concealed in the attacker's hand, and it would make its mark right between the girl's ribs... if Stacy didn't stop it.

Tick. Tick. Tick. Stacy could hear the clock now and feel the press of its urgency as she pushed herself to act. This wasn't anything like her murder, far from it in fact in both location and method, but it didn't make the pressure of the thing any less. If she'd been alive her throat would have been closing up, her breathing agitated, her knees quivering, and panic would have overtaken her at witnessing the scene unfolding. She wasn't alive, there were no airways to close up or joints to quiver, her whole being simply felt slightly off balance which was something she was more than capable of pushing past.

It catches the attacker and the girl off-guard when the knife flies from the attacker's hand, ringing out across the pavement as it skitters into the dark. But losing the weapon is only ever a small setback, Stacy knows that much. The girl of course doesn't, she's still stuck in a monkey-brain panic loop frozen to the spot.

"Run." It's the only word Stacy whispers, the only word short enough that she can push it through into the existing world. And frankly, it's the only word she needs.

Shivers run down the girl's spine, the loop breaks giving her the clarity to make a decision. It's an easy choice. Not questioning if the voice was real if she was imagining things, or how long she has to get away, she turns heel and runs for the main street. They are hot on her heels; she doesn't look back though.

It's lucky, the side street isn't long, a short dash to the main street. Even though the girl can't manage to scream, and her attacker isn't far behind, she doesn't need to worry because the street is busy. There are people all around, she melds into the crowd losing the attacker, their method of escape has become hers. Pure luck.

That's enough though, Stacy thinks, luck is more than enough. If it means another girl gets to go home alive, if it means nobody died that night, Stacy's happy to rely on luck. Except she'd never been that lucky, not when she was alive.

Werewolf Road Trip

Mica was propping open the van's hood with a stick, trying to figure out what was wrong with the car's engine. Monica rolled her eyes at him, grumbling about radiators and other junk. Sid and Harley were complaining about the heat, and how it was all one or the other's fault. John had stomped off into the forest in a huff and Judy busied herself with reading a book. To anyone passing by it would have seemed like an ordinary group of twenty-somethings on a road trip, but this was no ordinary group of people.

In the forest, John could smell the fear of tiny, delicious rabbits. His eyes keenly honed on the ever-so-small tracks his prey had left, and as he drew closer, he could hear the thumping of their hearts. He quickly lunged into the rabbit hole precisely grasping one of his quarry by the foot in his jaws. Successful, he withdrew from the hole and padded back towards the road.

Back at the van Mica stopped looking at the engine when he heard the rustle of leaves from the forest. He turned to see a wolf emerging from the trees...

"John, where the hell have you been?"

Slowly the wolf changed form, turning into a man; rabbit still clutched in teeth.

John removed the rabbit from his mouth and quickly cracked its neck, then wiped the small traces of blood from his mouth.

"Well, I figured with the van broken down I might as well go for a little hunt."

Monica turned to him and rolled her eyes, "And if we'd fixed the van and left while you were gone? What would you have done then?"

"Sheesh Monica relax, Mica's hopeless with cars no way you would have been able to leave without me. But hey, if you had, I know where the next stop is, I would have hitchhiked there and met up with you."

"Hey, I'm not hopeless." Grumbled Mica, turning back to the engine.

"Sure buddy." John patted him on the back as he walked past, then knocked on the van doors, "I'm cooking rabbit stew, anyone want in?"

"How much rabbit are we talking?" Replied Jane, not looking up from her book.

Sid and Harley, distracted from their fight, pulled open the van door to peer at John- their eyes gravitating towards his hand which was holding up the rabbit. Their faces dropped in disappointment.

"It's only one rabbit? Couldn't you have caught more John?" Harley sighed.

"And it's so tiny, how exactly would you make enough stew for all of us?" Added Sid.

"Just one rabbit huh?" Jane clicked her tongue in the back, still reading.

"Well, I don't see any of you lot going out and hunting for food." John was not impressed.

"Hey everyone calm down, we're trying to work here!" Yelled Monica from the front of the car, "You know so we can continue our road trip."

"Whatever." The others responded.

Softly and to himself, Mica grumbled, "take the whole pack on a road trip, it'll be fun, and you'll bond. Yeah right, at this rate we're all just going to kill each other."

"Do you want me to look at it, Mica? Because that might make this whole thing go faster." Monica sang out through the window; Mica could hear her hands nervously drumming away at the wheel along with the continuing argument in the back.

"No, I've got this. It's my van, I think I know what I'm doing." He rolled his eyes then immediately regretted it as smoke billowed into his face, an acrid smell curling up his nostrils. "On second thought, maybe you could hop out and help. But get someone else to sit in the driver's seat in case we need to test if it's working."

"Sure, sure." Monica's hand waved lazily out the window as she turned back to look at their fellow travelling companions. "Sid, Harley, quit arguing, would you? I need one of you to take my spot while I help Mica with the engine."

"I'll do it!"

"No, I'll do it!"

Monica vacated her seat at speed as her bickering packmates surged forward to try to claim the driver's seat. Sid's hairy arms stretched between the seats creating a barrier, but it hardly phased Harley who lunged forward to crawl over him.

"I'm the better driver." Harley poked her tongue out blowing a rasp-berry into Sid's face as she tried to hoist her right leg over his shoulder.

"You wish." He growled, releasing his left hand's grip on the passen-ger seat to use it instead to pull Harley down.

"That might take a moment." Monica sighed making her way to the front of the car, shaking her head as Sid and Harley continued to argue. "Those two will fight over anything."

"We should have made them draw straws and left the loser at home." John piped in, returning from the back of the van with a portable stove and pot to cook his rabbit stew.

"I should have just made this trip on my own." Mica seethed under his breath as Monica leaned over him to look at the engine.

"That wouldn't have been very future alpha of you." Monica teased before changing to a more serious tone, "I think I see the problem. Back up so I can fix it, would you."

Mica stepped back, mildly disgruntled. This was supposed to be a fun, educational road trip across the outback, a nice change of pace from the everyday. Instead, it was turning into a migraine. 'I should have made them all catch a plane and meet me there for the ceremony. This was a terrible idea.'

"So, you going to go full wolf for the ceremony, or you got something fancy to wear all picked out?" John asked while skinning the rabbit, the fresh smell of raw meat and blood was a welcome change to the smoke smell that'd been clogging Mica's nostrils.

"Haven't really decided, not really sure I should even be going through with it." Mica drew a hand through his thick brown locks, sparing a glance at Monica who dutifully worked away at the engine now he'd conceded it to her. "Don't really feel very alpha material right now."

"You'll be fine." John chucked the rabbit into the pot whole, discarding the fur into the shrubs. "Harley and Sid are driving us all a little mad, but you'll be fine. Don't you think so, Mon?"

"Hmm," Monica grunted in reply.

Mica chuckled; the pep-talk wasn't helping.

"I don't think she's really listening; besides I can't even fix my own van up. How am I supposed to lead a pack?"

"Well, you don't really have to." John poured water into the pot before firing up the stove, clearly, he didn't think they'd be moving anytime soon. "I mean, we're a pack and you'll be in charge, but it's not like a big deal. You can still let everyone be the way they are, maybe you'll step in and solve an argument occasionally... not between Sid and Harley, but you know reasonable stuff."

"Jeeze, thanks for the vote of encouragement." Mica laughed; John wasn't completely wrong. "Now I feel like maybe Dad just told me to bring you all on this trip, so he didn't have to sort out Sid and Harley."

"You might be right; I don't think anyone could stop them arguing." John slammed a lid onto the pot and grinned, "You want some of this when it's done?"

"Sure, should be enough for the two of us." A little bit of the tension in his head eased, Mica squatted down next to John. "So did you really intend to share, or did you purposefully go out and just get one rabbit?"

"I resent your implication there, Mica." John guffawed, "I had every intention to share, it might be lacking in meat but the stew will still be hearty."

"Sure," Mica rolled his eyes, letting out another small laugh. "You're not worried Monica will be done before the stew is?"

"Nah, even if she is we'll still have to sort Sid and Harley out before we can go. That'll take at least three hours, plenty of time for me to finish my stew." John joked but it wasn't too much of an exaggeration, Mica could still hear Sid and Harley tussling for the driver's seat.

It was nearly night when they were able to hit the road. Monica slept in the back, oil and dirt smudges on her clothes, while Jane rode up front in the passenger seat nose still buried in her book. John sat in the back between Sid and Harley who were grumbling about not getting to drive and being deprived of stew, he kept the two separated to avoid another full-blown wrestling match in the car. The road was quiet aside from the noise of the wind.

"This isn't so bad." Mica sighed, flicking on the radio to fill the strange silence now descended on the van. 'Might not be such a bad trip after all.'

Train to Nowhere

The train was going fast, so fast I could barely believe it. Scenery dashed by before I could register it, everything melded into one big whoosh of wind and colour. This was it, this is what I had been dreaming of, the adventure, the excitement, all the fantastic new experiences and it all would begin here on this train. I had barely hoped to dream that I could actually do this, that I could go out and see the world.

"Lilia, come back inside... it's not safe to stand on the platform." Lionel called to me from the carriage doors, the wind twirled my skirt around as I looked at him.

"But Lionel the wind is sooo nice out here, and it feels so much more real than just looking out a window."

"That's nice and all but we are on a moving train, please come inside where it is safe,"

"Aww, you're no fun Lionel." I pout a little before conceding to his pleas and going inside. The carriage is not exciting, but I suppose it is rather beautiful. We are in a private carriage for our journey, Maurice says it's not wise to travel openly and that at least we should separate ourselves from the common folk, but I feel it would be far more interesting if we were in a shared carriage.

"I see you've re-joined us Lilia, get bored of the wind and bugs?" Maurice is prickly, he's always making snide remarks and chastising me. However, I don't dislike him, he is after all the whole reason I am on this trip, getting to realise my dreams.

"No, Lionel begged me to come back in so I did."

"What a good girl, always doing as you are told." Then again sometimes he really irks me.

Rather than responding to Maurice I take my seat, I have learnt over the past few days to never engage with Maurice as his tongue is quicker and sharper than mine. Lionel on the other hand, who takes a seat next to me, is a soft-hearted and kindly fellow. How Lionel and Maurice became acquainted I don't think I'll ever know; they are both rather secretive about their lives before the journey.

It's a rather special journey, Maurice is an emissary for the King with the duty of escorting the Princess to the Kingdom of Florine where her betrothed is. That's as far as my knowledge of Maurice goes, even the Princess won't tell me anything about him though she is quite happy to share details about herself. Princess Maureen loves birds and kittens, she tends to flowers in her spare time and her favourite colour is 'cream', not that any of it is useful information but at least it is something.

I know what people must think of me, I could see it in the eyes of strangers as we boarded 'she must be some kind of noble or a skilled fighter? Perhaps a mage.' But they're all wrong, I'm just a simple girl from the countryside. Really Maurice only let me come along because the Princess needed company, I was the lucky girl who got chosen from among the masses in a lottery. It doesn't sound great, but for me it was amazing, being chosen finally gave me the chance to leave my home and see the world, it was the opportunity of a lifetime and I'm the lucky one who got it.

My eyes slowly, drowsily open. I must have fallen asleep; I take note of my surroundings.

"So, it wasn't a dream," I breathe a sigh of relief as my eyes roam around the train carriage, at least it is a sigh of relief until I really notice my surroundings. There's nobody in the carriage, there's no feeling of movement, the train has stopped, and my companions are gone. "What's going on?"

I rise from my seat and search under the seats, in the overhead compartments, all the luggage is gone—even mine. "Where did everyone go?"

My feet take me to the doors, I step out on the platform, and I see the outside world. However, we're not at a station, it is just an empty landscape all around except for a few trees and some rolling hills in the distance. What has happened? Where are my companions? Did they leave me? My head is pounding as I try to figure things out. I search in my mind for some possibility, for an answer to all my questions. My palms feel sweaty with nerves and my heart is racing.

What should I do? I collapse on the hard floor of the platform; the metal is hot and my skirt is getting dirty with dust and grime but I don't care. This was meant to be fun, an adventure, but now it's simply lonely. "Where are you guys? Lionel, Maurice, Princess Maureen!" I cry out into the void.

They weren't my ideal travel companions, but they were the ones I was lucky enough to have gotten, and they were the only people I knew so far from my home. Listlessly I look back and forth hoping to catch a glance of someone, or something that might be able to help me.

Slowly it gets too hot to sit on the platform and I resign myself to searching the other carriages; there are six in total so maybe the others are in one of them? Or if not perhaps there's somebody else who I might be able to confer with. Inch by inch I search each carriage until finally I come to the final one and that's when I see it. Nothing could have prepared me for this, not in a million years.

I had read about this in books, in magical tomes when I had thought about learning to be a mage, but I had never thought to actually see it. When I'd given up the idea of becoming a mage, I had firmly put the thought of coming across something so archaic from my mind. "So, this is what happened,"

There in front of my eyes lies a pulse bomb, I and the train for some reason have been transported to a void landscape with no chance of returning to the true realm. Why did this happen? Why am I the only one who was transported here? Is this to be my life from now on? Several questions come to mind as I stare at the arcane device, long since banned from use. It has an eerie, pulsing blue light to it and there's a strange kind of humming noise emanating with each pulse.

I search my mind to try recall something from the books I'd read on them, but the knowledge has long since left my mind, been forgotten to make room for more pertinent information or so had been my thinking at the time. Now it seemed foolish that I'd given up on ever considering the study of magic, but it wasn't as if I'd had the funds to properly pursue the study so truly there wasn't much point arguing I'd made a mistake in my previous life choices. No, I just simply had to accept matters for what they were; I'd been transported to another world along with the train via pulse bomb, probably during the night, and now for the moment I was utterly alone.

Briefly, I wonder what this means for my travelling companions and events in the true world. Are they safe? Were they thrown from the train when it was transported? If the Princess doesn't make it to Florine in time for her wedding does that mean our kingdoms will go to war? I nervously chew at my cheek while considering all the possible ramifications until a flicker of movement outside the train jolts me back to the problem at hand.

"Just because this is another world doesn't mean you're alone Lilia," I whisper to myself, turning my back to the pulse bomb, "and if I'm not alone, then maybe I can get home. Or at least find something to eat."

It's just a different kind of adventure, that's what I tell myself as I leave the train to face the unknown head-on.

Prayer Power

"Could you guys maybe hurry it up and defeat this dragon?"

Olympia's forehead is drenched in sweat, her brow knitted in frustration.

"It's a little hard, you know you can't really" Octavius ducks as the beast's tail swings at him, "rush these kinds of things."

"Yeah, it's not like we can just" Dalia pauses to line up her shot before firing an arrow into the dragon's flank, "snap our fingers and be done with this!"

"No, I totally get that. But I'm running out of prayer power here and that means we really need to get this over and done with. You know, before you both become vulnerable and excessively easy for it to, oh I don't know, KILL YOU?" With each breath, Olympia feels her power drying up, the Gods can only loan so much strength to a mortal.

"Right, yep, copy that." Octavius sprints up the dragon's back, hurdling over the spines and slashing downwards with his sword, tearing a gaping wound into its neck. "I'm just not sure that the dragon is 100% on board with that plan."

The beast roars as it rears up onto its hind legs. Before it can complete its threat a gleaming arrow burrows into the exposed flesh of its belly.

"And done." Dalia rests her bow, a smug grin plastered across her face.

"About time," Olympia huffs as she collapses onto her knees, "you couldn't have maybe wrapped it up a tad sooner?"

"Don't see how we could have managed that, what with it being just the two of us," Octavius grunts, as he plunges his sword into the neck wound he'd made, and prises a scale free. "Now if your Gods could see to guiding a few more competent souls to our aid, that'd be a real help."

"Yes, because it's not like I contribute enough," Olympia grits her teeth, resisting the urge to roll her eyes as she focuses on regaining her breath.

"You do plenty." Dalia pats her on the back as she saunters past to retrieve her arrows from the dragon's corpse, "Octavius, doesn't mean to be an arse, he just can't help it. That said, we really should look at recruiting a few others to help with our hunts."

"Only problem with us recruiting is then we have to split the purse, but if they're workers of the faith they'll do it for nothing." A series of loud grunts follow Octavius' comment as he continues to prise free more scales. Olympia shoots him a dirty look but holds back her tongue. "Plus, with the recent surge of dragons, bounties don't pay as much for them, so we've got to harvest as much of the ruddy things as we can to try make back the cost of armaments by selling to the alchemists."

"You're not wrong," Dalia hums to herself as she inspects an arrow pulled from the creature's flank, "It's not exactly cheap maintaining our gear for dragon hunts."

"Perhaps we should pursue more profitable prey then? Rather than straining my abilities further by adding to our ranks? Or trying to take advantage of the faithful." Olympia feels mildly better, her strength must be returning, she rises to her feet to help assist her comrades. "And then perhaps we could also reduce our laundry expenses because I find it near impossible to get dragons' blood stains out of my robes."

They take the time to contemplate that matter in silence. Olympia with Dalia's assistance drains five vials of blood from the beast whilst Octavius manages to pry another ten scales from its hide, unfortunately, their endeavours result in the girls' clothes being stained and Octavius' sword blunted. Still, when they return to town and cash in the bounty it is barely enough to cover new arrows for Dalia, they sell the parts gathered to the Alchemist which covers the rest and allows a nominal amount of profit.

"I'll be taking the lion's share," Olympia decrees as they sit down in the tavern to split their earnings, "part of which I'll be donating to the temple as always. Wouldn't want to fall out of favour with the Gods and have my powers dry up."

"Of course, wouldn't want that." Octavius bitterly grumbles as he begrudgingly splits the coin and pushes the larger pile to Olympia. "Hopefully though one day we won't be beholden to your prayer power."

"Hopefully," Olympia bows her head before getting up, there's no time to waste she must make haste to the temple, "but for the moment you, as we all, are beholden to the Gods."

Traitor

Blood dripped off Lynel's hand even as he brought his fingertips to his lips.

"She has such *sweet* blood," he flicked his tongue across his digits and grinned.

Donnel tried not to gag as Lynel reached down, plunging his hand once more into Princess Elena's chest.

"How could you do this?" Donnel was barely aware of Lisa's angry screams, of how the chair shifted as she angrily wriggled, thrashed, and strained against the ropes holding them in place.

"With ease," Lynel smirked as he strode forward to smear his bloody palm across Lisa's face.

It was no use, Donnel expelled the contents of his stomach onto the floor as Lynel moved to rub the Princess' blood onto his face.

"Tch, tch, how disgusting Donnel. And you called yourself her protector."

"You scum bag, traitor!" Lisa screamed as Donnel continued to throw up. "Princess Elena took you in, cared for you. She--"

"Abducted me. Took me away from my home and all I ever knew?" Lynel sneered, suddenly grabbing Donnel's hair and yanking his head up. "You're fools, disgusting little rats. And she was the worst of all."

Lynel let go of Donnel's hair rather quickly as the lad threw up once more. He simply couldn't stop throwing up, he could feel the Princess' blood sticking to his skin and clinging to his hair. It was too much.

"Now which of you would like to follow your beloved Princess into the hereafter first?" Lynel brandished his hand out in front of them, from the corner of his eye Donnel could see the blood coating it; glowing red and bubbling with heat. It brought back the memory of what had occurred just mere minutes ago; waking up from a drug-induced sleep just in time to see his supposed friend plunging his fist through Princess Elena's chest. Bile rose in the back of Donnel's mouth again as he recalled Lynel ripping out Elena's heart and devouring it, recalling how utterly useless he was in his Princess' hour of need… how utterly useless he still was.

"We don't care!" Lisa raged against Lynel, somehow able to keep her spirits even though she was just a chambermaid. "Do what you will, you cowardly traitor. They'll find out what you did, you'll never escape the castle alive. For spitting on the Princess' favour your head will roll!"

"So, you first?" Lynel chuckled, the heat from his hand so intense that Donnel could feel it, "Very well, but just so you know, I don't need to escape the castle. Elena wasn't my first stop; the King is dead too and the town has already been infiltrated. This isn't a petty attempt at revenge, it's a coup, I'm taking the throne for myself."

"You bas—" Lisa didn't get to finish her sentence, Donnel winced as he heard the gurgle of blood rising in her throat. He couldn't watch, not again, he closed his eyes and let his body continue to wretch as he waited for his own end.

"Pitiful really," He could hear Lynel approaching, he expected it, "Princess' protector and all you can do is watch her die, then puke your guts up. Old friend you are a tragedy but don't worry I'll put you from your misery."

It was fast, painful but fast. The heat seared into the flesh of his backside mingling with the splintering of the wood from his chair being pushed into it, an excruciating pain erupted across his whole being as Lynel's hand plunged into his body, and then it was over.

Fae Feast

Gossamer wings create coloured reflections in the room like stained glass, as the sunlight filters through them from their perch on the windowsill. The scent of honey and warm milk wafts from the stove, as a gentle song is hummed.

Shimmer's slender feet tiptoe in a tiny dance as she moves about the kitchen, gathering dishes to place in the sink. She sniffs at the air to check if any of her cooking is done before darting to the cupboards to collect a series of bowls.

Mice skitter across the floor trying to stay out of her way, dodging to-and-fro as she kicks up her heels in an unknowable dance number. Some scramble their way up the curtains making for shelter on the windowsill next to Glimmer who sits silent and still watching it all unfold. Others make a game of it, playing at Double Dutch with Shimmer's feet as the ropes.

A half dozen bowls of varying colours and sizes, Shimmer places them each out on the table with no care for which goes where before retrieving spoons to rest beside them. The honey smell is shifting to something almost akin to caramel as Shimmer whisks the mixture of milk from the stove, it's piping hot and full to the brim but still, she dances as she carries it to the table.

Hot honey-coloured droplets splash over the sides to rain down on the floor, the remaining mice cease their games to duck and weave out of the way none keen on being burned. There's a notable sploosh sound as more mixture overflows, landing with tiny plips to make sticky stains on the floorboards.

Glimmer's eyes carefully follow the flow of liquid as Shimmer pours helpings into the bowls, some she fills to practically full while in others she places barely a drop. The last pour of the mixture is sludgy instead of flowing smoothly like the previous pours, it resolutely sticks to the pot while select droplets splash into the bowl below. Twelve drops, once those twelve slushy drops are in the bowl Shimmer prances away with the pot.

There's a knocking at the door, a strange clackity type of knock against solid wood. Glimmer twists their head just slightly to look towards it, and the mice beside them scatter as their wings shift in place. Reflections in the room darken and brighten with the motion.

Shimmer pays no heed to the knock; she instead busies herself retrieving glasses from another cupboard and placing them next to the bowls. The glasses are oddly shaped, some long flutes and others round and short, each one is filled with the same liquid though as Shimmer pulls a jug from the icebox. It's clear like water, filled with dozens of varied flower petals, and from it comes the slightest scent of rose and apple.

Feather enters from the hall, having let himself in after his knock went unanswered. Pink and purple plumage speckles his arms which he crosses in front of himself while waiting for Shimmer to notice his presence. Glimmer waves from their perch but offers no interruption.

A wave of heat blasts from the oven as Shimmer opens it, she pulls huge trays of cookies out marvelling at the shapes they've formed. Red ones with bright white speckles in the shape of tiny domes, green ones with streaks of brown curling-like leaves, and pink ones with bright yellow centres whose edges have bulged out in strange bumps. She breaks her humming with a trill of glee at the sight, placing one tray on the counter as she hops her way to the table with the other.

She makes a ring of cookies around each bowl, varying which types she uses for each of them and giggles with excitement as she finishes. Clapping her hands in delight she catches sight of Feather standing there, she beams at him gesturing with her hands to the great spread she has prepared. He rolls his eyes derisively but takes a seat, nonetheless.

Glimmer alights from their perch to join him at the table, purposefully avoiding the bowl with sludgy mixture in favour of one full of smooth elixir. They do not touch any of the spread, even as Shimmer takes her place. Three seats remain vacant, so the present company waits.

The sun's light departs bringing the room into darkness aside from the soft glow of fireflies rousing from their hiding places to come play outside the window. Still, they wait in silence for their remaining guests. The honeyed milk in their bowls is long since cold.

Feather's fingers thrum against the wood of the table impatiently as even the mice depart for somewhere to sleep. Shimmer still smiles, her feet still tapping out a beat beneath the table. Glimmer sighs, staring into their glass with unquenched desire.

It is many hours past the setting of the sun when the remaining three guests arrive. Without knocking Lustre, Fawn, and Bramble mumble apologies as they enter the abode. Hurriedly they take their seats and strain to make apologetic smiles as Feather glowers at them.

Glimmer doesn't wait for words to be said, now that company is present, they clasp their glass tight and raise it in a toasting motion before drinking down the beverage inside. Ravenously they devour cookie after cookie, pausing only briefly between each bite to dunk them in the honeyed milk.

Shimmer laughs at Glimmer's antics before shrugging and taking up eating herself, hers is a more restrained approach of soft nibbling at cookies and sipping her drink. When she has finished the first red cookie around her bowl, she takes up a spoon to scoop a mouthful of honeyed milk. She licks her lips for any clinging drops, humming happily at the taste.

Bramble whose wound up with the sludge bowl opts to push aside the bowl in favour of only partaking in the cookies. Fawn who sits beside him pushes some of her cookies to him, content to have just the honeyed milk herself. While Lustre downs their glass before getting up and retrieving the jug to refill it, Glimmer shoots out their hand to beg their glass be refilled too.

It's a happy meal, cold from the waiting but still delicious. Slowly as they dine, conversation starts up and even Feather finds himself partaking in the laughter.

Another year will pass before they dine together again and then it will be Glimmer's turn to prepare the meal, for they must each take turns.

The Wood

Long leporine ears, soft and smooth like velvet twitch under the rays of the morning sun. Tiny sounds, the beating of a butterfly's wings, the thumping heartbeat of a field mouse, whisper secrets of a world unseen. Whisps of lavender waft by on the wind tickling the senses.

Rows upon rows of flowers stretch across the field, Lupinus of pink and blue creating swirling images for those looking down from high. A trilling caw from ravens circling above piques the interest of the ears, swivelling slightly to pick out where it's coming from. She can't quite pinpoint it, so she continues on through the flowers, almond eyes focused on what lies ahead.

Brushing her hands gently against the flowers and their leaves as she goes, dew drops cling to flesh briefly before bursting. The scent of the flowers whisks up into her nose with each inhale, replacing the wisps of far-off lavender. A deer in the distance catches at the corner of her eye but is gone as a rustling in the trees spooks it.

The creature is following her, she is certain of it now. It is staying out of sight, hiding most of its movements among the tiny sounds, keeping to the shadows of the tree line. She does not fear it, this is expected. What it wants is for her to turn, to go back to the place where the lavender grows and stay far away from the wood.

She won't go back though; she must go into the wood. This is the only way home, the creature if it blocks her way will have to be dealt with. A big breath in through the nose takes in the aroma of Lupinus flowers, and a big exhale follows as she prepares to slow her breathing.

One step at a time, she sheds unnecessary items as she grows closer to the wood. First, the shoes upon her feet kicked off, her toes curl happily against the soil relishing the soft feel of it. Next the flowing skirt she wears, her nails puncture the fabric and rip it into rainbow-coloured threads as she strides forward, what remains underneath is the overhanging fabric of her shirt just enough to cover her underclothes from showing. Finally, her hat, which is a delicate removal, she eases the straw accessory over her leporine ears careful to go slow and steady so as not to risk hurting herself.

Free from the tatters of the outer world she runs forward towards the wood, towards the home she longs to at last return to. The wind rushes against her velvet ears as she flattens them back against her head charging ever forward, the sound of it covers up all other noises but her sense of smell will make up for that. As she breaks into the wood leaving behind the flowers, new scents dance into the air, fungus and moss, rot and decay, dampness, and musk.

Her senses feel keener here amongst the wood as she brings herself to a stop. There are no formal paths here, this is a wild land, and although it is the way home and she has walked it before she must be careful she does not become lost. She surveys the clearing she finds herself in, straining her ears for the sound of the creature through the many tiny noises. It must be waiting for her, watching her from somewhere she cannot see, but for all her efforts she cannot hear it right now. That is troubling.

Tentatively she takes a step forward, ears perked listening for the slightest change in the landscape and eyes focused on the way ahead. Loud internals muffle her hearing, the thundering beat of her heart, and the subtle shift of air as she inhales and exhales. Still, she must continue.

Every shift in the foliage sends a tremor down her spine, it's unpleas-ant, her whole body is on edge waiting for the creature to strike. The further into the wood she goes the more she sinks back into her old self, her toes curl as she shifts her weight from her heels into them. Her nose twitches picking up a peculiar almost metallic scent, she can feel her muscles coiling ready to run at a moment's notice.

Long deep inhales, she can monitor her surroundings and keep calm if she trusts her nose. The scent isn't easy to keep track of though, not amongst the odours of the wood and its inhabitants, it takes a great deal of focus to pick it out from underneath the mixture of aromas. Leaning into her sense of smell means less attention being paid to her ears, they droop slightly but still retain some rigidity of alertness as adrenaline courses throughout her body.

With how heightened her senses are inside the wood it shouldn't be possible for her to be caught off guard, but even with all the advantages of her long leporine ears and keen nose, the creature retains the advantage. It bursts out from the canopy, a blur of fur and claws diving towards her from a singular blind spot directly behind her. She moves out of its path, the sound of branches cracking from its weight her saving grace, the creature's breath is hot upon her neck as her muscles reflexively force her to run forward.

She can't look back, now that she's run, it will be chasing her. Not that she needs to look back, she can innately sense it behind her, sometimes it's so close she can feel its breath against her flesh again. Over branches and logs she bounds, her toes flicking up pebbles and dirt as she charges through the wood.

A river lies ahead, she pays no mind to the obstacle it could form. In a single motion, she leaps the major distance across the stream splashing up water as she lands in the shallows and continues her way. Looming trees with low-hanging branches threaten to slow her down but she ducks and weaves around them, she mustn't deviate from her path lest she loses track of the way home. If that happens, she will be at the creature's mercy.

Darkness claims the wood, the further in she goes the harder it becomes to see what lies ahead. Adrenaline keeps her going through and pushes past any thought of hesitation that may cause the creature to gain ground. She can hear its heavy breathing, mere inches behind her.

It isn't visible but she can feel it as she nears home, deep in her bones she senses it's there. She tumbles forward, curling her long legs into her chest and covering her head with her arms as she rolls along the ground. The air around her whistles with a swipe of the creature's claws, but it won't catch her now, the ground slopes beneath her aiding the roll and guiding her forward down into a burrow.

Home. Dirt skitters down after her peppering her ears and hair as she unfurls her body and stretches out. It is still dark but now she can wait for her eyes to adjust, now she is out of the creature's reach, deep in the underground of the wood. She breathes a sigh of relief, home at last.

Leap of Faith

The mist billowed at her feet, tiny tendrils of it snaked their way between her ankles as she breathed in deeply. There was nothing to it. All she needed to do was just take a step. She scrunched her eyes closed, feeling her brow wrinkle as she did, and let her breath out.

Just a little step.

Her heart hammered away at her ribs; every inch of her body was fighting against her. There was nothing to worry about. She just needed to move her foot forward and picture the mist solidifying beneath it. Simple.

Curling her fingers into her palm, she could feel the scrape of her nails as she clenched her fists. Her whole body trembled as she pushed through, willing herself to move forward even as she kept her eyes closed.

There was nothing there. Her foot touched emptiness, she bit down on her lip, this was no time for hesitation. Despite the fact she felt naught but void beneath, she followed through pressing her weight into that foot and urging her body forward off the edge.

Her heart nearly plummeted, she swayed slightly off balance as her back leg lifted off the ground and finally, there was a sense of solidity under the first. That was the easy part. She didn't open her eyes, not yet. Painstakingly she began the trek forward, blocking the feel of the gusting breeze surrounding her from her mind.

One step, then another.

At last, she felt it, proper ground. It was firm with no give beneath her, she breathed a sigh of relief as her back foot lifted off the pillowy mist she'd been walking on and touched down on the earth. Finally, she opened her eyes.

"You did it!" Her classmates whooped and hollered, rushing up to congratulate her with pats on the back. "Good job, Veronica."

She smiled, trying to keep herself upright as they jostled her about. She wouldn't look back though, she might have made the crossing but it'd be a long time before she tried something so reckless again. Her knees felt like buckling, but she couldn't let on how much it had fazed her... not here, not with them, not if she ever wanted to be a magus.

Musings

Emerald Hills

Rolling emerald hills stretch out as far as the eye can see, bespeckled with rich verdant trees, cradling effervescent meadows of flowers in the valleys between them. Lilting bird songs fill the skies as large flocks migrate southwards, dozens of little feathers floating free to be lost amongst the sea of greenery below. The sun burns bright just at the edge of the horizon, bringing orange, pink and purple hues into the pale blue above as lazy clouds drift and shift.

Truly there was no other sight like it, anywhere else in the world. As the sky darkens, birds vanish from sight and a conglomeration of bats rise in their place, dark bodies and chittering sounds searching out any insects that have come out for the evening. An owl makes brief appearances between the hills, lofting from one collection of trees to another seeking out whatever prey it might find amongst the flowers.

It is a natural place, but not a wild place. There are no signs of farmsteads or houses, no livestock milling up and down the hills. All there is are the creatures to which it belongs, though who can know for how long that will hold true.

In the morning light, sunbeams bring fresh dew drops into glistening light. Young deer venture from their hidden homes amongst the trees to graze alongside boars and other beasts. Soft cotton-tailed rabbits bound amongst the flowers as birds warble and perform loops in the sky above.

Snaking between the emerald hills, barely a murmur giving it away, clear blue water flows in a tender stream. Creatures of all sizes wander to its banks lapping up much-needed sustenance, some wade in trying to catch darting quick fish whose scales glimmer in the light as they hurry along the path of the stream. A lonely falcon circles above, diving down lightning fast before rocketing upwards its prize reflecting light between its talons.

This is the domain of the beasts; quiet, secluded, brimming with life uninterrupted. It is here the most majestic of creatures can be found, for so long as this place may remain a sanctuary it shall be. White flanks shimmer from the sunlight, silver manes flicker in the wind like delicate strands of silk, ivory hooves thunder across the ground yet barely leave a trace, and sparkling horns of diamond refract each beam of sunlight that passes through them creating bouncing rainbows across the landscape.

Once they could be found across the world, now it is only here in this sacred place that they will be found. If their final home should be tarnished who is to say what will become of them; will they return to the earth's embrace and become mines abundant with jewels, shall they shed their ivory, silver, and diamonds to become simple horses, or perhaps they'll take to the distant sea and vanish into the waves to become something entirely different. Who can say? For the moment they are as they always have been radiant and pure.

What will happen if human feet touch the ground of these hills? With all their luscious beauty they may very well hold deep magic. Would the resplendent emerald shift to tarnished bronze or faded copper, should the trees recline, shrivel up and die, the many coloured flowers wilt, and the stream run dry? Is just one step into this blissful abode all it would take to corrupt the natural tranquillity? Perhaps the question itself doesn't matter, what matters is if the result would be worth it and surely it cannot be. A natural place such as this surely deserves to remain untouched, unblemished for as long as possible, protected from the taint of the outside world so that the creatures residing within it may continue with their lives unaware of the dangers outside their home.

From atop a mountain, surrounded by pure white snow the emerald hills are visibly nestled in a valley down the other side of the mountain.

While they stretch as far as the eye can see, past them lies yet more mountains; a ring of tall rocky guardians protecting this last sanctuary by presenting a truly daunting climb for anyone to even venture a glance and an even more perilous journey for those who may seek to disturb it. But just a glance is worth it, a slither of a peek at this wonder of nature and its majestic inhabitants leaves the whole body gladdened.

Burn

I walk through the fire, my skin blisters from the heat as flickering orange tendrils lap at my flesh. My lips crack with dehydration as I keep them sealed shut, holding my breath tight as smoke pollutes the air. The air is thick and heavy, ash dancing on the breeze, I squint trying to keep my gaze focused in front of me whilst reducing the amount of debris flying into my eyes.

My head swims with dizziness as my lungs scream for oxygen, I hold my right hand out in front trying to feel for where the flames stop. When I reach the other side my eyes sting with the lack of moisture, I collapse onto my knees gasping in what air I can get. Smoke still chokes the air, wisping in my lungs and bringing forth coughs as my hands press to the ground.

It stings, everything hurts, heat still swirling beneath the skin. I don't know when it happens but everything turns black as I struggle to keep breathing.

When I wake I can still smell the burning, the ash, the heavy smoke. Yet I can see none of that, my vision is dark with speckles of light bleeding through, I can't hear the crackle of flames though so perhaps I'm no longer at the fire or maybe my hearing is playing tricks on me. There's a low electrical hum that I can detect, but who is to say it isn't just the static of a dying mind?

I want to feel my face but movement in my hands and feet feels stiff and tingly, just tensing my fingers to claw at the ground is a trying task. The ground below me isn't dirt, it's surprising, cautiously I try again to clench at that which is below me. It's soft, a little scratchy, fabric, not soil. Two of my senses can't be wrong, can they? Surely, I must be somewhere far from the fire now.

"..." Words die in a crackling rasp as I try to form them, my throat is parched. No matter where it is I am, the fire's ravaging is not yet healed. If only I could see.

For what feels like hours I languish in place trying to hear something that might help, but my body is tired before I know it, I've slipped under again.

Snippets of words rouse me from my second slumber, there's a prickle in my skin as if someone is standing close to me. I try in vain to bring forth some words, to move my limbs for attention, anything that might help me gain more clarity of my surroundings.

"No ID yet on our John Doe here." "Their condition is holding stable." "Must have been crazy to walk through that fire." "Not like they had much choice."

I hear the same sentences over and over again as I drift between consciousness. My eyes, I've decided, must still work. There's an odd kind of itch to my face, and a stickiness I can't place, I may not be fully able to feel it because of painkillers being administered somehow but I'm sure there are bandages and bindings on my face, possibly all over my body. These must be the reason my vision is dark save for some speckles of light breaking through, if I could just work up the strength in one of my arms, I might be able to pull them down a bit and free up my sight.

The doctors are shocked when they next come in, my eyes no longer bandaged are able to take in their figures. I can't see properly, there must be swelling or some other side-effect from the burns I endured that's keeping them mostly sealed but I will take what I can get. The walls are white, the lights blindingly bright, and the team of doctors is larger than I expected.

"You're awake?" One of them asks, his tone sounds young and there's a nervous rasp to it.

I can't answer with my voice, I've tried numerous times to form words but they just won't come. So, I nod my head, or at least I'm hopeful I'm managing to nod.

"Fascinating." This one has an older voice; it rings with curiosity. "To think you'd survive, and then to go a step further and wake up even with your body completely ravaged by the flames. Truly remarkable."

"They might still be suffering brain damage; we can't account for anything just yet." A feminine lilt. "We should book in for some scans."

There's much talking about me, but very little talking to me. It is no better than when they thought I was asleep, they still ignore me. Who knows for how long I will have to endure this?

Days go by; I am scanned, poked, and prodded with little concern about if I am comfortable. As I am speechless my wants are ignored. I gain back a small amount of control in my hands but it is far from enough to write, no other methods of communication are opened to me. Perhaps they like it this way.

I focus on trying to recall the life I had before the fire, and my reasons for pushing myself to walk through it, but everything is hazy. It is as if the smoke that curled inside my lungs from the fire has drifted up to my brain and taken permanent residence, clouding my memories. I wonder if this is all that is left for me, to be a guinea pig with no means of communication and no way of recollecting my past. Is all that I am now a husk of who I was before, is all that remains burnt just as my skin?

The pain is immense when they remove my bindings, the cloth does not part easily from my skin; it sticks and clings taking chunks of pink flesh with it. I may not have words but even my damaged throat can howl and wail in torment as they swab me down with anaesthetic and some magic salve. Each and every inch of my being stings with the treatment, and I whimper as they make me stand and wait for it to dry.

"It'll be done soon, and you should be glad there'll be no more bandages. You've reached the stages where we can begin treating with magic, in a month or two you might be able to go home." The young one is my attendant through this torture, he tries to soothe with his words, but they bring no comfort to the pain. "You're lucky, most people would have died trying to walk through dragon flame."

Is that what I did? Is that what the fire was? I can barely recall the walk now and have long since given up on recollecting the cause for it. These thoughts sift to the surface for but a moment as searing pain brings me back into the present moment.

Enchanted ice is being spawned around my trembling legs and it burns, it burns frightfully, I feel as if I am back in the fire. Treatment they call it, but I am reliving trauma, it feels as if the flames are crawling along my skin once more. If not for its heavy nature, and how it is wrapped so completely around me, the trembling ache accompanying the pain would bring me to my knees. As it is the ice holds me upright.

It feels like years go past as I endure the treatment; my skin feels alien to me when I touch it. In appearance I look better, the magic does wonderfully at cosmetic change, but when I run my fingers along my arms, I can feel lumps and bumps all along it whilst it appears smooth. My memory doesn't improve, the smoke in my mind remains firmly lodged even as they finally discharge me.

"Don't go walking through dragon flame again." A chirpy young woman who only recently joined the team calls out behind me as I leave.

I nod in answer, I'm sure I never wanted to walk through the flame. It must have been an option of last resort.

The shoes they gave me are a little large but they numb the prickling sensation I get as I walk, when I go barefoot no matter the surface it feels as if a thousand tiny needles are poking into my soles. My other clothes from the hospital itch against my skin, the fabric is tight and doesn't breathe well, but of all the things they fixed my throat never made a full recovery so I couldn't complain.

Where will I go now? I know not where to return to. Vacantly I stare out at the landscapes stretching before me; a resplendent city lies ahead, the coast to the east, and to the west, there is a burned land. Perhaps the land to the west was once a lush forest, a city, or a farming village, who can say from so far away?

Absentmindedly my feet choose the direction on their own, my mind is too busy trying to push past the everlasting pain to think about it until I'm too far along to turn back. I'm heading west, to the land as burnt as I was, perhaps there I'll find answers?

Branded

The sky is awash with birds in flight, their colours cannot be made out against the harsh sunlight, but the shapes and patterns are magnificent. I stretch my hand up, it feels as if I should be able to touch them, I know I cannot possibly hope to reach them. They are no more touchable than the clouds which look ripe for plucking out of that lush blue.

Alone with only the birds overhead for company, I am left prey to my own thoughts, and thoughts can be savage beasts. Much as I try, I cannot avoid those ponderous beasts that plague me. No matter how I daydream and speculate the same matter keeps pressing forth and hounding me. The problem with the predator in one's mind is that it is unavoidable; no matter what you try it cannot be escaped.

Five days now, five days that I have spent lying in this field, five evenings that found me trudging home. It has been torturous; no matter how little time I spend there it always feeds the beast, creating tumultuous nerves and stress within me. And still I have not yet found a solution, never mind how long I spend in the field wracking my brain for a way out, I can barely breathe some days as I am overcome with fear of the unknown.

There is no more time for deliberation, I am out of time to try and avoid this matter. All those days spent in the field, and I have nothing to show for it, no solutions and no escape. So, it has come to this, I can feel the nerves twisting in my gut like a knife.

I wish I could blame someone, but there is only myself to blame. If only this day could be like any other, if I just close my eyes, I can almost see the sky filled up with birds and pretend that I'm back in the field with only my own thoughts. Tears prick my eyes as I step forward, here goes nothing.

One's rank cannot be changed, not by inheritance or marriage or any number of things. It is permanent, your assignment is forever. That doesn't mean you can't do whatever you like to improve your life, but it means you'll always be marked and looked at a certain way.

The rank system is more like a skill assessment, a career advisement that is branded into you for eternity.

No matter if you pay heed to the results of your examinations or not, but either way it will be marked into you. The brand is scorched into one's skin and sinks so deep it marks the bone - even in death, you shall be marked by your rank. It is this that I wish to escape, but it is impossible - the only way out is to leave the land and to leave is an option I cannot take.

Solemnly I must accept my fate.

The blessed iron burns unforgiving into my bare skin. I cannot contain my moans of agony as my flesh contorts and sears under the brand, as I feel it becoming etched into my bone.

Burn The Witch

This was sooo not how I had planned for my 18th birthday to go down, hiding from people with pitchforks and torches, not even close to my party plans. You know this is typical, I plan the most awesome birthday bash EVAR and something just *has* to ruin it.

I mean I worked my butt off at a part-time job to save up money for decorations, catering and music. I could have just conjured the décor and enchanted the kitchen to cater for me and given my friends a talent potion so their band played well. BUT nooo, I worked for it because using magic is dangerous and shit like this happens if you do.

Ugggh the universe is so out to get me. I mean of all the things to get caught out on I get caught for having a fictional book on my shelf that apparently only appeals to actual magic practitioners, WTF universe. I mean what are the chances that my BFF's cousin's dad is a witch hunter? Is in town for my birthday, and decides to drop off my BFF and her cousin to my party? That has to be like a million to one chance.

All I did was try to be a good host. I asked him if he'd like to come in for a refreshment because it's polite manners, and *of course* when he comes in the first thing he sees is this book.

This is so not fair, Stacy's 18th might have been a disaster but this is a-a-a-a CATASTROPHE. Worst birthday present, ever.

Oh shit, I can hear them chanting. Sheesh, people, you've known me forever, glad to know that being best friends means nothing once you are revealed to be a witch. Thanks a lot Mum for giving me magic-worst inheritance ever.

"Burn the witch, burn the witch, burn her."

Oh puh-lease people, get a new line.

I mean 'burn the witch' that is so archaic. And burning a witch isn't even effective. Panic, when you are burning, has proven, over Wiccan history, to be an amazing survival instinct because 95% of the time it helps the witch pull off a long-distance teleportation spell. You would think that regular humans would have caught onto that by now.

Anyway, even though it's not effective I guess I still don't want to risk being part of that 5% who do die in fire. I should probably try and escape, that would probably be a good idea. God why did Dad have to be away on business this week? He'd totally have memory wiped all those people and fixed things... still not like I can wait for Daddy to show up and save me.

Balloon in the Sky

Adrift in the clouds, nothing but air and endless blue.

Bobbing along, up and down, up and down.

Wistfully travelling miles over time, moving ever so slowly to an undetermined destination.

Not a care in the world, sailing across the vast ocean of sky.

Back and forth, back and forth, the wind rocks gently.

Cruising across the sky, no reason why and no goals ahead.

Up, up and away from it all.

Nothing to do but rise in the sky, rise up and sway along.

Winged creatures flying past, flock disrupted just for a moment.

Squawks and screeches fill the sky, the only form of company.

Still drifting, endlessly drifting through the sky.

An untold story adrift in the clouds.

-

BANG

The drifting ceases and falling begins, softly and slowly.

Swaying on the currents of the wind, being cradled on the fall down.

Down, down, down, keep going down.

The air is sight and sound, touch and taste.

Soon enough this fall will cease.

-

The boy tugs at his father's hand to draw attention as he points straight up at the sky, there is a red balloon bobbing along and then before long, there is a red balloon falling to earth as it has finally burst. He watches in fascination, no matter how his father tries he will not budge for he must see this spectacle. And at last, the remains of the balloon gently come to rest on the ground.

Falling

In this moment she is an angel, a halo of light and wings of white silk. Her hair billows softly and gently caresses her face, her skin the closest to white it has ever been.

There's a soft light to her eyes, a little spark that burns brighter the closer it is to going out. In this moment she is the most serene, the most beautiful woman in the world.

Even with scarlet tears streaming down her cheeks, even with the soft purple tinge to her lips, she looks peaceful.

There's something in her facial features, something that says "This is it I've reached my goal, now nothing matters".

-

"Why is this happening? I'm not done living yet!" I scream in my mind.

I am trying to scream out loud, but the air has been sucked from my lungs and no noise leaves my throat. My limbs want to flail but I'm scared to move them. Instead I will my body to hold form.

Stretching, the only movement I will allow, my hand reaches out. "Save me," that's what my hand is saying, "Please, Lord, save me."

I'm scared. So scared. My eyes begin to bleed and tears mix into the blood. Slowly my vision blurs, I can only just make out my fingers which still stretch and plea for saving.

My silent pleas fall on deaf ears, my tan skin feels blue. Is this truly how it is all going to end for me?

-

He watches her fall from his position on the ground, a flurry of hair and white fabric plummeting to the earth from on high. She is not moving, it is a corpse.

"That one is already dead," he thinks.

"WHAM!" The body crashes into the ground a short distance from him. He ignores the fallen body, attention caught instead on the trace of a city in the sky, vision trained on a slight silhouette in the clouds.

Battered Old Photograph

Elsie was an old woman, getting near 90 years of age; she had wrinkles and frown lines. Her long white hair thin and wispy, and her smile extremely crooked. She had lived a long life, not an ideal one she thought but a long one.

Back when she had been a little girl she had dimples, rosy cheeks, and a million-dollar smile. Her parents had doted on her something fierce, always dressing her in nice dresses and shoes with buckles and ribbons. That had been a happy time; childhood had been good to her.

Her parents always wanted the very best for their only child. All through elementary school she had been spoilt and everyone could tell, but then times had gotten hard for her parents and while they wanted her to have only the best of things it just wasn't feasible. When she entered secondary school there had been cutbacks. She had been sent to a public school and given a uniform. It was a downgrade but not wholly unpleasant as her parents focused more energy on spending time with her to let her know she was loved.

The later years of her adolescence had been markedly more difficult than childhood. Her father had gotten lung cancer and her mother was trying her hardest to earn enough money for his care and for them to live on. This meant further cutbacks, no new clothes or uniforms and no sweets or toys- clothes had to be mended by Elsie if they got torn. And so, for her final years at school Elise had worn the same old uniform that was a size too small and had patched up tears and a crooked hemline, she took a bagged lunch and stayed late to finish her studies.

This had all been bearable until her father passed away just before her graduation. After that, Elsie didn't feel like going on to further study, even though her mother offered to send her (money be damned her mother still wanted the best for her). No, rather than go to college and study, she chose to start working at a diner. It was working there that had let her meet Teddy.

Theodore Montiv was a joker, he was a happy chap and he made Elsie smile. He mightn't have been more than a dish-boy, but he was sweet, and kind and he took good care of her. She'd been so happy when he proposed, been downright giddy when she told her friends she was getting married.

They'd only been married a couple of months when the war started, only had a few more weeks together before Teddy had been conscripted. She'd only gotten to be Mrs Montiv for barely a year before she became Widow Montiv.

Now she'd been Widow Montiv for about 67 years and she was lying on her deathbed, cradling her most treasured possession. It was yellowed around the edges and creased down the middle, there was a tea stain on the back and a slight rip on the bottom left corner but boy it was a lovely memory.

'I'll be with you soon Teddy.'

Troth

Lucy circled him, he would be hers - never mind his engagement to her sister.

It didn't take long to corner him alone in the kitchen, the door locked to keep pesky intruders out.

Slowly she strides towards him, her right palm caressing his face as she blows softly against his ear.

"I. Want. You."

He pulled back, roughly hitting the benchtop with the mid of his back.

"What are you talking about?"

He went to manoeuvre around her, but she pounced onto the chopping board slamming her heel onto the benchtop, blocking his way with her exposed leg.

"Don't run Noah, I know you've always wanted me."

"Maybe a long time ago, but I am betrothed to your sister and I love her."

He darts the other way as her other leg comes down, trapping him in between. The soft red of her lingerie becomes visible, and he's stuck trying not to look.

"Forget her, Agatha is so boring."

"No, I gave her my troth, I will not break it."

Lucy couldn't help but giggle, troth - he was so old-fashioned.

"Look at you and your fancy old words. Clearly, you're aroused," she pulls her dress up, fully exposing the lingerie beneath. "Don't deny yourself, Noah."

"No, I will not break my troth." He pushes against her leg. The force caused her to wince, reluctantly she pulls back her leg, not wanting it to bruise.

"Please, Noah, I want you."

Jumping down from the chopping board before he can reach the door she rushes up, embracing him from behind, pushing her breast against him.

"No, you don't. You want Aggie to be miserable. You only want what you can't have."

Forcefully removing himself from her embrace he strides to the kitchen door, unlocking it he storms out of the room. He will never be hers.

Primal

"Eugh" I repeatedly hit the punching bag, ventilating all my anger... all my resentment, all my pain. I transfer all of it into energy, and channel that into my punches, allowing it all to seep out and break away from me when I hit the bag.

There is nothing worse than self-loathing; there is no pain someone can push onto you that rivals the torture of constantly being at war with oneself. The trouble with self-loathing is that it always ends up twisted and deformed. It moves into depression or worse a complete breakdown of self. I hate myself.

Or at least I hate some form of myself. I hate the part of me that leeches onto others, and I hate the me that is weak and pitiful. Most of all I hate the part of me that is always self-certain, that is positive that is...

"AUGH!" My right leg flies up, and solidly my shin hits the bag centrally. The bag moves just that once.

The constant battle I fight with myself is only made worse by the constant disgust I have for others, whilst simultaneously being jealous of them. In this world, or at least within my mind, I am an anomaly.

Nothing about me seems right, or in place, no part of me feels like it is correctly designed - not even my legs of which I am so proud of for their long elegance, or my hands which I could never live without. I feel out of place, out of time, as if I was never meant to be where I am.

Only when it is me and the punching bag do I feel as if I am truly there. For when there is the bag in front of me I can remove everything else from my mind, and then all that is left is raw emotion.

"Nahhhgh" I am constantly changing with each punch- left, right, left, right. When I am punching, no part of me is dominant, all that I am is primal. Evolution does not challenge me when I am focused. I can be an ancient beast and merely seek the primal urge of blood lust for as long as I want.

If I punch and kick for long enough, I forget all my worries. I become awash in happiness, and sweat, I become someone who I do not loath but seek to be.

When all is over I have stripped away all of the guttural trash and layers that have weighed me down, and I am left as the base. I am what I was always meant to be, I am what I started as. I am a clean slate, and an empty path.

However the base cannot last forever, for once the sweat dries and I wash away my work, the layers come back- thicker and heavier than before. Once I am naked and can see all that I truly am, I must realise that I am no longer able to go back. There is only forward and, there is no base for me to return to. When I reach that realisation the self-loathing increases.

"HYAAAAAAAAAA!" My fist hits pure emptiness for there is no bag there for me to punch. Without the bag, I cannot shed, and when I cannot shed, I am forced to bottle up my anger, my rage, my blood lust. And should all be bottled up for too long it will explode and once again I shall be primal.

Anxiety

It's a dozen tiny spiders scuttling inside my skull, tingling tiptoeing on my brain. A vice around my heart and an anvil on my chest. There's itching beneath my skin that won't vanish no matter how much I scratch.

But it's not a big deal, nothing to cry about, no stress. At least as far as everyone else is concerned.

To me, it is a nagging thought, a twist in the gut that refuses to let things settle. I can't help but think about it over and over again until my heart rate is elevated and I just can't sit still. There's got to be something I can do about it.

I'd like to release the tension by crying, taking a long hot shower, and just sitting there in myself. Screaming might do the trick too, in a nice wide-open space with nobody around for miles. Neither of those are an option right now, I'm supposed to be doing other things... I'm not supposed to be panicking over something so irrelevant.

Sometimes the nagging thought generates a sound like a fuzzy low-frequency static only I can hear, it goes along with the throbbing in my forehead. If I tell anyone about it though, they'll just tell me to relax – it's nothing to worry about, everything is fine.

I feel like a failure, some great big anomaly of a person. Why does it have to be this way? Is this really such a foreign thing to them? Is it wrong to be worried about this, are my feelings invalid? I don't know, I don't think that can be right. It all just makes me want to cry more. But if I cry, if they see me cry, it'll be worse.

When the issue resolves it's a weight off my chest, a chance to breathe clearly again. The throbbing lessens, my muscles relax, and best of all I don't have to listen to the remarks anymore. Nothing lasts forever though; another problem will rear its head soon forcing me to bottle myself up again. But at least for now, for a moment, I can feel normal.

Rules

Everything is about survival. That was rule number one, rule number two was everyone is out for themselves—trust no one, only do what is good for you—so Kelly had to ask herself why hadn't she just stuck to the rules?

She'd made the rules as a strict guideline when at the tender age of ten her own mother had abandoned her. The rules made things simple, they kept her alive. It wasn't an easy trade off but she'd take living with nightmares over being dead any day of the cycle. And now with her fingers barely maintaining a grip on the ledge she was resolute that the rules were right.

Jhona was prettier than any sunset or newfound object, light would reflect a rainbow of colours when it touched her hair. As soon as Kelly laid eyes on her she should have run, the second she'd felt her lips mimicking the large smile on Jhona's face she should have forced them into a frown, there were lots of things she *should* have done. But it did not matter because in that moment she had been spellbound.

"Hi, I'm Jhona!" She'd said her name effortlessly, her voice a soft chime even in the midst of the dust bowl. "What's your name?"

"Kelly." From that first meeting the rules had started to scatter to the wind—rule number four never let anyone know who you are, they'll hurt you—but Jhona's smile had been warm and her skin smooth as she shook Kelly's hand.

"That's a nice name, Kelly. Do you think you could help me? I'm a bit lost." The flutter of her eyelashes had been utterly bewitching paired with how her tongue softly licked her lips.

"I could, maybe, where are you trying to go?" Kelly's brain had screamed at her to remember the rules, but she tuned it out lost in the purple hues of Jhona's eyes. Rule number three never agree to help anyone, offer assistance, or aid without first figuring out if there is something in it for you.

"Krystal. I'm trying to get back to Krystal, you see I was kidnapped and dragged out here but I managed to escape and now all I want is to get home." Jhona's hands were so soft and smooth, her fingers inter-twining with Kelly's were so warm. "You'll help me, won't you, Kelly?"

"I—" Kelly gulped, her brain felt like mush as all thoughts of rules vanished replaced by the sensation of Jhona's hands clasping hers, "I will."

-

Krystal, the oasis city, was no easy place to reach. It was three days journey, by foot, to reach the outskirts and from there the perilous trek through the maze of ruins tended to persuade even the most desperate to keep away. Kelly had visited the outskirts before, even ventured into the maze a short way, but she'd long since decided it wouldn't be worth the effort...and yet one look from Jhona and she found herself willing to do almost anything.

They'd grown close during the trek to Krystal's outskirts, at least Kelly had convinced herself that they had. For warmth they had cuddled together at night the first night, and the second night Jhona had intro-duced Kelly to kissing. So Kelly was certain it couldn't be a mistake to disobey the rules this one time—rule number ten never break the rules.

"Here we are." Kelly had tried to hide her disappointment as Jhona looked in wonder at the outskirts, "I suppose, this is where we part ways."

"Kelly," She'd been ready to head off, to begin aimlessly wandering the lands once more, but when Jhona's melodic voice called out to her there was no going back.

"Yes?" Her hoarse voice cracked with desperation as she gazed longingly back at Jhona.

"You can't leave me yet," Jhona's hands were still so smooth as she grasped Kelly's, "these are but the outskirts, we still need to make it to Krystal."

Perhaps Kelly should have taken that as a sign, should have known all Jhona cared about was reaching Krystal, but in her mind all she heard was a plea for them to stay together.

"Okay, I'll take you all the way to Krystal." Hesitantly she pressed a kiss to Jhona's forehead and pulled her into an embrace. "I won't leave you." Rule number five never get attached.

"Thank you, Kelly."

That night Jhona had opened Kelly's eyes to a whole new experience, it was greater than kissing, and with that simple act Kelly had known she would break the rules numerous times just to remain with Jhona.

-

"Jhona, pull me up!" She'd cried out at first when the rusty rungs of the building had given out under her. "Jhona?"

For those first few minutes as she hung there she was actually worried something had happened to Jhona. Her voice grew gradually weaker as she wasted energy screaming out for help, trying desperately to figure out if Jhona was okay. Then she'd spied it from the corner of her eye, the rainbow hues of hair were a dead giveaway as a figure gently proceeded to scale down a sloping ruin in the distance.

"Jhona?" She rasped in disbelief as the figure vanished from sight. This was it, she'd been left to die...worse she'd been coerced into this deathly maze, bewitched into helping. Kelly gritted her teeth as the rules reaffirmed themselves in her mind, she'd been made a complete and utter fool. "Jhona!"

Ephemeral

This wasn't how today was meant to go. I just wanted a normal birthday, no weird family zoo trips, and no experimental dinners. All I wanted was a nice time, a small dinner with my besties and a little dancing at the club. Maybe a hook-up, but definitely not this.

I can feel hot tears on my skin, my throat burning from yelling to no end. There's also the feeling of blood, hot and sticky across my abdomen. Why? Why did this happen to me? And, of all days, on my birthday.

There's nothing to be done for me, I can feel my body going cold; I'm dying. It's a bit surreal when I leave my body, watching its final breaths and the light in its eyes go dull. I'll admit it takes a while for me to fully realise what's occurred.

Looking at the bloody mess that was me, I only really start to realise what's happened when I manage to stop sobbing. When I dry my eyes, it just clicks into place. I'm a ghost.

It's incredibly frustrating.

"Hello!" I don't know what I'm expecting, but it seems like the thing to do.

"Uh, hello! Is anyone here, can anyone hear me?" It's useless, I can feel tears prickling in my eyes... it's funny to think that while my body is dead I can somehow still create tears in this ephemeral form. I'm not sure how long I stay there, in the place where I died, but eventually, I leave.

I can't really tell if I left because I decided to or if my body just moved of its own accord. Slowly I float over my hometown, the place that had made me feel safe and happy... the place where I was murdered. Is anyone looking for me?

-

Somehow, I found myself at Michelle's house. My best friend, who hadn't shown up for my birthday celebration. She was the responsible one; the one who made sure everyone was hydrated and didn't drink too much. But, she wasn't able to attend... maybe if she had I wouldn't be dead.

"Why weren't you there?" I yell at her as she puts on her makeup.

"Why can't you *see* me?" I feel tears starting up. She, of course, can't hear me and finishes up her eyeshadow before leaving the room. "Don't you know I'm DEAD!"

Still no reaction, I follow her around the house. Then her phone rings.

"Hello, this is Michelle." She sounds upbeat, but in a moment her face drops. "No, I haven't heard from Liz. No, I couldn't make it last night."

I can't hear the voice on the other side of the call, but from what Michelle is saying and the mention of my name I can guess it's about me.

"Of course, if I hear anything I'll let you know. Don't worry, I'm sure Liz'll be home soon." Michelle wraps up the call, she looks a little disturbed but shakes herself out of it before leaving the house.

As soon as that door closes behind Michelle I am alone once more. It stings, this terrible feeling, knowing that I won't be going home again and that soon enough my friends and family will know that. But will they ever know I'm dead?

It nags at me. This thought, this disturbing thought, that my body won't ever be found. Maybe, I should go back there, to the place of my murder, and wait to see what happens with my body. I consider it, but I really don't want to. Just thinking about my lifeless, bloody corpse is enough to bring me to tears.

-

I can remember it all so clearly, the lead up to my death.

It had started a week before my birthday, a long week of arguments with my mother.

"MUM, I *don't* want to go to the zoo this year!" She was trying her best to ignore me, putting away groceries and humming to herself. "Did you hear me, Mum? I do not want to go to the zoo this year."

"It's tradition, Pumpkin." Her response was not desirable, I rolled my eyes and huffed.

"But, Mum... I'm turning 20. The big two-oh! I want to celebrate with my friends, and do adult things. Not go to the zoo with my brothers and look at the monkeys, before eating some weird concoction Dad's come up with." If it took begging on my knees to get what I wanted, then I would do it.

"But, sweetie-pie, it's tradition. We've done this every year since you were four." If only I'd just conceded and gone along with tradition, maybe I wouldn't be floating around as a ghost.

"So traditions are made to be broken!" Why did I have to be so stubborn?

"Fine, fine. Your father will be so disappointed." Mum conceded first of course, and perhaps with that my fate had been sealed.

"Yes, thank you. Thank you, this is going to be the *best* birthday EVER!" How wrong I was.

In no time at all it was my birthday, I'd been so happy to celebrate. I hardly slept the night before, nothing was going to bring me down. As far as I was concerned, no matter what, this birthday was destined to be perfect.

So, when Michelle called saying she couldn't make it, I brushed it off.

"You can't come out tonight? Really?" Talk about leaving it to the last minute, she called half an hour before pre-drinks and dinner.

"No, no, I get it. No, that's fine. I know you'd come if you could, don't worry I get it." Of course, I was a little pissed that she couldn't make it. But her boss had called her in for a last minute shift and I knew she needed the extra money for rent. Instead of fuming about her absence for the whole night I decided to start drinking early, and one mojito quickly turned into five.

My other friends weren't as responsible as Michelle, they were fun and free and down to party. Together we got extremely buzzed whilst enjoying a light dinner, I was adamant this would be a night to remember... in a way it still was.

What possessed me to go home with a total stranger? Probably the fact that he had these deep, soulful eyes and that I'd lost track of my friends hours ago. In my blissed, drunken state I couldn't even comprehend what a bad idea this was. Maybe, things would have been different if I'd instead gone home with the nice girl I'd been dancing with earlier.

It's too late to think about what could have been after all the deed has already been done. I'm dead, murdered for who knows what reason, and stuck in an ephemeral body.

It takes two days for my mother to file a missing person's report with the police. Two days, in which I flitter between houses, screaming at friends and crying when nobody sees or hears me. It's torturous to be stuck in this ephemeral form and unable to reach out to anyone, from what I can tell there aren't any other ghosts hanging about either, I'm trapped here all alone.

I follow Mum around on errands after she leaves the station, there's really nothing to do about it. She's trembling a bit, she always had a good sense for things, she probably knows deep down that I'm dead. Poor Mum.

Of course, I can't do anything for Mum or for anyone else. I can't even do anything for me, I vaguely recall movies saying ghosts were just spirits with unfinished business, but I honestly can't comprehend what that could be. Maybe, I need justice? I think I read something like that, or maybe I saw it in a movie or television show? The ghost moves on because its murderer is apprehended.

That doesn't seem too unattainable, then again it's not like I can tell the police who killed me... they haven't even found my body yet.

Weeks go by, recently my older brother has been accompanying Mum to the police station.

"What do you mean there's no news?" He screams at the officer, "Haven't you tried tracking her phone?"

"We've done that, sir. Unfortunately, it seems her phone was left at the club. We've been talking to everyone she knows but there's no clues yet as to where she went." I can see my brother's face going red as the officer says all these things. My mother has tears streaming down her face as she sobs into my brother's arms.

And here I am, a ghost, just watching. I feel like screaming at the police myself.

"I didn't leave my phone at the club, my killer must have taken it there!" Of course, it's no use, no one can hear me.

"She wouldn't have just run off! I'm telling you something happened to her, you need to look harder!" Poor Paul, my big brother looks ready to cry as he continues to scream at the officer.

He doesn't get any answers, Paul and Mum are sent home with no further information. They look so sad. I wish I could touch them and comfort them. Alas, all I can do is follow them, unseen and unheard.

I've been dead for about two months now, just floating around the town waiting for something to happen. I make a habit of visiting the police regularly; waiting to see if any news about my case comes up. And low and behold today they found my body.

I haven't seen my body since that day, the day I became a ghost. It's started to degrade, I feel like vomiting as I watch them analyse it. Thankfully, they don't take long to cover it up and wheel it away. They don't know that the body is mine, not yet. But soon I'm sure they'll run tests and reveal that it is me. Finally, my family and friends can stop worrying about me... of course, now they'll start mourning me which is probably more upsetting.

Still, even with my body located it doesn't seem like I'm going to move on. Which leaves me with a new question, will they be able to find my killer?

I can't really remember his face anymore. I was so drunk when it happened. It's funny, I remember the first stab into my gut, and I remember just being confused. In my drunken haze, it had taken a while for me to realise what was happening, what I was feeling, of course as soon as it had clicked into place I'd begun screaming- not that it helped.

Maybe, if I'd started screaming earlier or if I'd been a little less drunk, this would all have been avoidable. What's past is past though, and all I can do right now is watch the police work.

I follow the leading detective to my parents' house; I watch my mother break down into sobs and my father's face go pale. Listening to the exchange I can hear the officer asking my parents to come to the station tomorrow, my poor parents are going to need to see my body. Bile, I can feel bile rising in my throat as I picture my parents looking at my rotting corpse. It's funny how I can still feel and react as if I was alive.

So caught up in my thoughts I don't notice the detective leave. I finally shake my head free of those disturbing thoughts, only to notice the door is closed. No problem, I'm a ghost after all. Floating inside I watch as my father dials the phone, who is he calling?

"Paul, it's Dad." I wonder if Paul can hear the break in Dad's voice on the other side of the phone.

"It's about Liz. The cops just came by, they've found her... she's dead." Dad has to stop talking, he's sobbing so hard, I've never seen him like this before. Paul must be saying something, or maybe he's crying too? I wish I could hear the other side of the conversation.

"Okay, we'll see you soon... you're sure you're okay to tell Evan?" Paul must have offered to tell our little brother. I wonder who will tell my friends.

"Thanks, Paul. See you soon." Dad hangs up, I can tell he just wants to cry. Mum is looking at him with such sorrow, I can't bear to keep watching. So, off I float, away from my family.

How do people manage to organise funerals so quickly? The police released my body after a couple of days, all in all, it's only been a week since they found my body. And yet here I am floating overhead, watching my own funeral.

It's sad. Everyone dressed in black, my closed casket, the police officers outside and my family saying goodbye. I wish they could see me, wish they could know I'm here with them.

"Mum, don't cry. C'mon, I don't want this." I find myself mumbling during the speeches, everyone is so sombre.

All of my friends are here, crying. It's a mean thought but I'm kind of glad they're sad, maybe if they'd stuck with me throughout the night I wouldn't be dead. Michelle is walking up to the stand to speak, I wonder what she will say?

"Liz was a great friend. She was really generous and sweet, always had your back." Poor thing, I can see her hands trembling. "And it sucks she was taken from us, she was so young and amazing. She had so much to live for, so much she wanted to do. I wish I'd taken that night off work. I wish I could've been with her. Maybe, if I had she'd still be here."

Michelle goes on, a lot of platitudes are said but I'm not really listening. I wish she didn't have to be at my funeral, I wish she'd come out that night too. All I wanted was to celebrate my birthday with my friends, to have a fun night out. Instead, I wound up dead, a ghost watching my own funeral. Tears are streaming down my face, I could wipe them away but there isn't much point - it's not like my eyes will get swollen.

Two months have passed, and the police aren't any closer to finding my killer. There's no evidence, no murder weapon or DNA at the scene that isn't mine, the trail is cold.

"Ah, haha ha, haha ha," All I can do is laugh and sob, as the detective tells my Mum they don't think they'll be able to find the person behind my murder.

"The scene was spotless... other than the body. And the murder weapon seems like it was an ordinary kitchen knife, there's just no clues to aid us in even suggesting a suspect." Mum's in tears, a new sob racking her body with every word that leaves the detective's mouth.

"You've gotta be kidding me, you've got nothing? Nothing at all? You're just going to give up? She was *murdered!*" Evan and Paul have been staying with Mum and Dad, taking care of them, but still, Evan's outburst takes me by surprise. My little brother, he's always been so gentle, he doesn't have a temper. I used to tease him when we were little, and he never once blew up at me.

"We are aware, but unfortunately there's just not enough evidence. There are also no witnesses, there's nothing to guide us in the investigation." I feel a little sorry for the detective, it can't be fun having to visit a family in mourning and tell them you have no way of finding the person that killed their daughter, their sister... that you're calling off the investigation. He tries a few more times at reasoning with Evan before Paul comes from the kitchen and tells the detective to just leave.

"There's no point wasting your breath, Evan." Paul's calm now. He was bristling with anger when they thought I was missing, overcome with sadness when they revealed I was dead, and now he's calm. Big brothers are like that though, they want to protect you and when they fail, they get mad. Poor Paul, he probably even spent some time blaming himself, he's probably still mourning but acting strong for everyone else.

Now that I'm dead, I'm seeing all new sides of my family. Little Evan is full of anger, Mum who was always so full of gusto can barely get out of bed in the morning, and Dad who was always weird, trying out new concoctions in the kitchen, well he just goes to work and then comes home and makes a regular family dinner. It's almost as if they died when I did.

I've officially been dead for a year now, still alone.

My family seem to be recovering, at last, getting back to being themselves, though I doubt they'll ever really be the same again. It's painful watching them, I usually only go to see them when I feel really sad.

I used to miss being alive, but I think I'm finally getting used to this ephemeral existence. There are things I can do now that were never possible when I was flesh and blood. Still, it would have been nice to have lived for a few more years.

Sometimes, I'll see someone dying in a car crash or at the hospital. In those moments I find myself holding my breath, waiting to see if another ghost comes into existence... but it never happens, if other ghosts do exist then I can't see them. I know it's bad, but I kind of wish someone would die and join me here in this ghostly existence.

As a ghost, I don't need to sleep. I've seen my whole hometown now, every nook and cranny. Sometimes, I consider leaving this place, I consider going somewhere new. However, something seems to be keeping me here, I guess I'm tethered to this town.

It's boring, being a ghost. Maybe, it'd be fun if it was like in the movies. If I could move things, touch things, reach out to someone, then maybe it'd be all right. But, I can't so instead I just float around town, aimlessly.

One year, three months and five days. I can feel a sigh building up, and then I let it out. I'm beginning to think this is a unique kind of hell, which I totally don't deserve. Shouldn't those who are murdered, for no reason at all, get a free pass into heaven?

The horizon looks funny today, I don't think I've ever seen it look so angry... there's something about it, I don't know why but I'm certain it's a sign. It feels like this angry horizon is calling me, it feels like it's something only I can see, something for the dead, not the living.

I'm not sure when I started to float towards it, I'm not really sure if I want to see what this means.

Here at the point of the horizon, or rather the signal. I know what this is, I know what this horrific, angry signal is. My eyes, I can feel the tears welling up within them.

This is a murder.

Sobs and screams are twisting in my throat, leaving me speechless. Not just any murder, this is just like mine.

The poor girl is choking on blood, it's dribbling out of her mouth as the killer continues to plunge the knife into her chest. Poor thing, her face is wet with tears, I can see the life slowly leaving her. So messy, so violent, so traumatic and I can't do anything to stop it.

She's got more fight in her than I did, she's clutching and grabbing at her attacker's arms and neck. Trying so hard to live, I wish I'd tried that hard but I was so drunk.

"Uggh!" A final scream rips from her body as the knife is pulled from her ribs and her body flung to the ground. It's that harrowing scream that pushes me, I need to see her killer's face.

Before he runs off I move in front of him, and I see those eyes. Those deep, soulful eyes that had led me out of the club and off to my death, it's the same guy.

He walks through me, cocky and sure. I can feel goosebumps on my arms, a shiver runs up my spine. Should I follow him? I'm not sure, but from the corner of my eye, I can see an odd light.

Rising from the dead girl is a spectre, another ghost.

"Ha, ha, ahh!" I'm not sure if I'm deliriously happy or some kind of upset, but I'm laughing uncontrollably. The girl doesn't seem impressed, but I'm also not sure if she's really paying me any mind.

"What? What happened?" She's mumbling, and yet I'm still laughing. "I'm, I'm dead aren't I?"

Her eyes pierce me, it's as if she's commanded my ephemeral form to cease laughing.

"Yes, you are." There's not exactly an easy way to say it, but she seems to be doing better than I was... and at least now I'm not alone.

Her name is Stephanie, she just moved here for work. He was a co-worker of hers, he'd offered to show her around the town. How was she supposed to know that he was planning to kill her?

She doesn't have anyone here, her family live in a different state. This was supposed to be the start of her independence, she was going to get a cat and take up yoga. She's a mess for the first few days, she doesn't seem to get that we can't interact with anything but each other.

It's a lot of work, trying to explain to her that I don't really know what's happening. Telling her that I think we'll be allowed to move on if they identify our killer and we get justice, but the police have no leads and have already given up on my case so that might never happen.

Stephanie goes off on her own, I don't see her for ages. About a month later she comes looking for me. I'm lurking in my parents' house when she whooshes in.

"They found me! They found me!" She's so excited.

"That's good, at least now they can begin identifying you and let your family know." I can't be excited, I was excited when they found me but after all this time I can't get my hopes up.

"Don't you get it, they found me! They'll reopen your case, and this time they won't just give up!" I roll my eyes.

"Oh? What makes you think that?"

"This time there are two bodies. Two bodies over a year apart but killed in the same fashion. They'll look harder for him now, if he's killed twice then he might kill a third time." I don't really think it's much to get excited about unless they find something new at her murder, but I feign excitement for her sake.

"Right, yeah. I'm sure this time they'll find him."

-

Five years and they still haven't caught him. I would have been twenty-five if I'd lived. Five years and four more bodies, he's due to kill again any day now.

We're not exactly hopeful that this time they'll catch him, but I do wonder when the horizon becomes aggravated if this time, he'll get sloppy. You never know, he could slip up one day. And when that day comes, I look forward to finally moving on.

A Little Gothic, A Little Horror,
A Little Thrilling

The Chant

The moon was high in the sky; there was nary a sound to be heard until the chanting started. It was soft and melodic, and the wind carried it across the field straight into the village. Sleeping girls were roused by the barely audible song. Pulling themselves out of bed, enchanted by the whispered words, they headed out from their homes. The girls walked along the roads until they reached the field.

A soft blue light emanated from the rows of wheat, fireflies danced across the sky. The little girls walked into the field, following the light and the chanting, which was growing steadily louder.

In the centre of the field, a circle of hooded figures stood, the chanting came from them. As the girls approached the figures parted making spaces for the girls to enter. Once they were all in the centre the figures moved back into place, closing the circle.

The chanting became deafening, a wave of tiredness washed over the girls and in a single moment, they all collapsed. The figures removed their hoods, bending down each figure leaned over a fallen girl to open their mouths drawing out the very essence of the girls.

It was almost daybreak when the figures put their hoods back on and retreated to the forest. The girls in the field lay motionless. When the cock crowed and the farmers went out into the field the girls were still there. One of the farmers ran to the village to find the parents, another checked to see if the girls were still alive.

They had a pulse, but yet not even one girl awoke. No amount of shaking, crying, yelling, smelling salts or cold water could rouse the girls from their slumber. The families carried back their daughters and placed them in bed, wondering if they would ever wake again.

Some of the girls died in this state, some lived as their families found ways to deliver nutrients to them... though most died.

When the full moon arrived the living girls arose and walked out once more to the field, this time the hooded figures waited with arms spread wide and spare cloaks on hand. The girls were dressed in their own hooded robes and without a thought for their families, followed the figures into the forest... never to be seen again.

It All Started With A Letter

It all started on a dreary Sunday afternoon. The sky had never looked so grey and the wind was unusually chilly. Yet still, Reginald marched across the marshland to reach the Upton household, firmly gripping his messenger bag.

Marchess Hall, the family home of the Upton's was rather small as manor houses go, so when the pounding sound of fists against the oak wood door rang out it was heard by everyone. Lucille, the head maid, was first at the door the rest of the household close behind.

"Mr Herts, what can I do for you today?" Lucille batted back the children as she addressed their visitor.

"A letter, for Meredith Upton," Reginald wheezed, pulling out the letter from his bag. "I, I've been travelling for the past few days to get it here. The sender said it was urgent,"

"Lady Upton!" Lucille called out for the only member of the family not present in the hallway already.

From the depths of the house came Lady Upton, cheeks flushed and face aggravated. Without a word she came to the door and took the letter from Lucille's hands. Immediately her expression darkened.

"Mr Herts, please come in... Lucille, please prepare the special tea for our guest." Lady Upton took off into the house, beckoning Reginald to follow. Deep into the house, they travelled till they reached a study at the very back, as far from the front of the house as one could be in Marchess Hall.

"Do take a seat, Mr Herts," gestured Lady Upton, reclining into a sofa herself.

"Thank you, Lady Upton. But, I really should be going... unless you have a response you wish for me to take back." Reginald was reluctant to sit, the hard stare of Meredith Upton brought sweat to his brow.

"No, no reply necessary." In the corner of the study was a fire, and with gentle ease Lady Upton threw the letter onto it. "You must at least stay for a cup of tea. It's Lucille's special blend."

Despite the fire, Reginald felt cold. It was as if the chilly winds of the moor had taken residence under his skin.

"I, I suppose that would be okay." Lady Upton grinned at his response, like a cat that had finally caught the mouse.

"Wonderful." As the words left her lips, there was a soft knock on the study door. "Come in,"

Balancing a heavy silver tray in her hands, Lucille nudged the door open. Upon the tray sat an ornate teapot, a peculiar burgundy colour decorated in what appeared to be hunting scenes, and a set of matching teacups.

"Mr Herts," ever the ideal servant, Lucille placed the tray upon a dresser before serving the piping hot tea. "Lady Upton. Please let me know if you require further assistance."

Curtsying before leaving the room she gently pulled the door shut.

Reginald hesitated to drink his tea, there was something troubling about the depictions painted on the cups.

"Please, drink up, Mr Herts. I assure you, this is one of the finest tea blends you'll ever taste." Lady Upton hadn't yet drunk any herself. Her cup remained firmly grasped in her hands just centimetres from her lips. Her gaze was unnerving as if she could see into the very depths of his soul.

"Ah, yes, of course." Reginald lowered his gaze from Lady Upton's face before gently lifting the cup. The hot liquid left a tingling sensation on his lips, though it didn't really taste of much at all. "..."

Lady Upton's grin grew into a terrible smirk as Reginald tried to speak, she chuckled softly.

"Oh dear, is something the matter Mr Herts?" She feigned naivety as he moved his mouth, but no words came out, "What is it that's the problem, Mr Herts? Cat got your tongue?"

Reginald wanted to move, to exit the room but his body would not respond.

"Oh, poor thing," effortlessly she lifted herself from the lounge, snickering at him. "Dreadfully sorry, but we can't have anyone knowing that letter made it here. No, we simply cannot."

She strode over to him and draped her arm around his neck, taking a seat upon his lap, "But, before we dispose of you, I'd like to have a little fun."

Reginald's eyes felt heavy, his lids closed without him wanting to and slowly everything seemed to fade away. In that moment all he could feel was the cold touch of Lady Upton's lips against his cheek.

Blood Stained Carpet

There are plenty of fingerprints in the room, but they could be from any of the house staff. The candelabra that was used as the murder weapon has at least five sets of prints which suggests the killer is either a member of the household or staff to have been so confident in not wiping their prints clean. There were no footprints outside that were out of the ordinary; clearly, the killer had decided it was safer not to run.

Police detectives and private investigators alike puzzled over who the murderer may be, almost everyone had a motive. There are arguments over if the body was moved, the blood stains on the beige hallway carpet seeming to imply it as possible, but the blood spatter in the study definitely pointing to it as the scene of the murder.

And then the shovel was found covered in blood. Funny thing is the blood doesn't match the victim.

The police began overhauling the yard; holes were dug all over the place, revealing a series of skeletons buried under the Manor grounds. Private investigators started amassing theories about the murders.

Nobody could figure it out. Were they all committed by the same person? It just didn't add up. Some of the skeletons were older than anyone amongst the Manor household. And they still couldn't figure out who the murderer of the victim in the study was.

In the nearby town, citizens were speculating and spread rumours. The owners are cultists, the bodies belong to misbehaving servants; the grounds are haunted. Everyone had a theory but none could be proven. With all the bodies buried in the yard and the fact the murder in the study had the police stumped, nobody was too surprised when yet another murder occurred on the Manor grounds. Evidence, in police opinion, suggested it was carried out by the same person as who offed the man in the study. No one could solve the case, and every few days the body count went up - either with the discovery of more hidden bodies or a fresh murder victim.

Three years went by with no resolution to any of the murders. Investigators were scheduled for an annual sweep of the grounds when they found the bodies gone. None of the many skeletons that had been in the ground could be located. After a call to the morgue, it was confirmed the corpse from the most recent murder had also vanished.

It was a mystery nobody could solve, and that most wanted to forget. But, 50 years later, the Manor grounds murders reared their ugly head once more, and the plush new carpets that had been put in were dyed, rich crimson red.

Twisted Love

His hands were resting on her hips; her body was pressed against him. The whole world had stopped existing, to them there was only the low thumping of music and themselves. She had been there to catch him when nobody else was, she had been watching him over the years, and she had been waiting so long for this moment.

He had been oblivious. He'd chased all the wrong girls or perhaps he just hadn't been able to tell which ones were the right ones. Now he wanted her, even though she'd been there all along, he only wanted her now that he felt there was nothing for him. And she obliged. She, after all, had never been looking for another, she had only ever wanted him.

It's a twisted kind of love, she loves him obsessively and he loves her until the next best thing comes along. Then it's a noose, he hasn't been paying any attention to her, he's been trying to chase someone else. She still loves him but now she's mad. It doesn't take much for love to become lethal; it all just depends on the people involved.

Now his lips rest on those of another, his body pulling theirs closer, they are cocooned in each other. Her eyes see everything, his image burns into her retinas, she bites her lip and screams deep inside. He never notices the crack in the doorway, the thin pool of light, he's too entranced with his new lover to see her approaching with a knife.

She plunges the knife down into his back, again and again. The other one screams as his blood splashes onto them. He cries out in pain, he cannot look back to see who his attacker is. As she plunges the knife in again, she holds her voice, she will not let him know that she's the one killing him.

The new one screams for mercy as she finishes stabbing him, they are crying. Of course, she doesn't care what they have to say, they took him from her. Slowly she drives the knife into the new lover, twisting it in place before wrenching it out and driving it back in.

Water washes all the blood off, she towels dry and dresses before grabbing the knife and heading to the police station. The person who murdered her beloved should suffer after all.

High Tide

I stand stock still in the water. Heavy chains restrain me, the cool metal chafes my skin. This is it, I can't believe it, death is upon me.

Spluttering, choking, coughing, nothing helps. Water fills up my lungs, clouds my vision, and within a matter of minutes, it all fades away. It's over, I'm dead.

-

"Police report a body has been found chained to the wharf." News trucks cram the streets, and reporters are clamouring to set-up and get the scoop. The drama and panic of it all create the perfect cover for him to slink by and witness his executed plan.

I want to scream, "My murderer is there. That's him!"

Of course, I can't. The dead don't speak.

My poor body looks awful. All slimy, covered in seaweed and bloated from water intake.

Two days of heavy rainfall, if I hadn't been chained up when the tide had receded I would've been dragged out to sea. The police finally take away my body; I hope the reporters didn't take any shots of it... I don't want my family to see me like this.

-

Four months and they still haven't arrested my murderer. He visits the wharf every day, it's like he's mocking me, and thinks he's gotten away with it.

Each time the tide rises I relive my drowning, the water filling my lungs. And each time I see them I feel those chains clamped against my skin.

Why haven't the police figured it out yet? I need justice.

\-

Five years. Cold case, that's what the people say. I'm never going to get justice.

That person, my murderer, still visits the wharf, not every day but at least once a month. His face looks twisted and menacing, sometimes there's somebody with him. Why didn't anybody ever notice him? Why couldn't they realise this sicko killed me!

\-

I watch them. Watch them kissing and laughing. I want to scream, "RUN! Don't let him hurt you! RUN!"

But the dead can't speak, so I watch. Watch him slam the rock into his prey's head, watch him clamp a set of chains to the victim's limbs and drill the chains into the wharf. Then he leaves and I watch the tide begin to rise. Watch as another drowns just like I did.

Wolves in Human Clothing

After hours cooped up in the car, Lisa was ecstatic to reach her destination.

"Finally!" She exclaimed exiting the vehicle. Her guide had mentioned being uncomfortable staying in the village so she quickly turned around, thanking him in Spanish before heading to the accommodation she'd organised.

The village was quiet, it was a pleasant evening. There was a nice, cool breeze and the moon was high above, illuminating the sky. It hadn't been an easy place to find but Lisa was happy to have made it.

She was a little perplexed over how everything was closed early, and even more astonished to find nobody walking at night. The scenery was breathtaking, with lots of hills covered in lush green trees. However, according to her guide, who had dropped her off in the village, she would do well not to go exploring the hills. The guide had said something further on the subject but in a rush and at a whisper. Lisa's Spanish was shaky at best.

Her camera out, taking photos of everything her flash emitting a short burst of light. It was then she saw them; people emerging from the hills, approaching the village.

"Hola!" she called out in greeting. When they did not respond she went back to her photography. To her delight, a beautiful owl swooped out of the trees and landed on one of the rooftops.

"Amazing," Lisa remarked. She'd barely seen any wildlife since arriving in Spain, even livestock had been scarce.

'Click, click' she took shot after shot of the owl, not wanting to miss out on this opportunity. Then all of a sudden the owl took off, flying back to the forest of trees.

It was then Lisa noticed the light sound of growling. Turning around there was nothing in sight that was out of place... except for the people who had come up the hill and were milling around.

"I must be imagining things," Lisa said to herself as she resumed photographing the scenery. But then she heard a howl, looking around once more there was still nothing unusual to be seen. "It must be coming from the hills."

She went back to taking photos, but after a while, she felt as if she was being watched. Suddenly the pleasant cool breeze seemed malicious and cold, the moon's glow sickly and pale.

Looking around, the people were still there... though they did seem to have all moved slightly closer. Of course, people tend to move about so Lisa thought nothing of it, but as she went to return to her photos heard a low guttural growl and turning around was alarmed to see the people running towards her.

That's when it happened, the people's bodies seemed to rip apart and in their place were wolves. 'Click' Lisa snapped a photo, and then they were upon her.

The sun rose above the village, Alejandro had just arrived to pick up the tourist whom he'd dropped off at the village.

He exited his car; the American had said to pick her up from the village hotel, so he began walking. There wasn't much to see in the village, it was just your usual small town. Honestly, he'd been surprised a tourist wanted to visit this village; most people hadn't heard of it.

Alejandro was admiring the patterns that had been put into the cobbled streets when he noticed the smell. Looking up the village hotel was right in front of him, but the smell didn't seem to be coming from inside.

It smelt like rotting meat. Perhaps someone had left something out in the sun too long? Looking around the streets he couldn't see any signs of meat, nor could he see the American woman he was meant to be picking up.

He enquired inside the hotel to see if she was there, but according to the staff, it seemed that after dropping off her luggage the night before she had not come back after going for a stroll. Clearly, she hadn't paid any attention to his warning the day before. Alejandro thanked the staff, and it was as he was walking back to his car he noticed the camera discarded on the streets. Stopping to inspect it, the camera seemed in perfect working condition. Why would someone throw it away?

Dyed Red

Her gown was dripping red. What a pretty colour thought the man as he laid upon the floorboards, such a nice contrast between the scarlet on the aquamarine. He was feeling woozy, and rather faint, and it was getting hard to focus. But he could see her dress, and the colours as she towered over him.

"This is for Freddy!" he heard her scream, and then he stopped seeing and hearing and just being in general.

—

"This is Dr Leonard Melwet, he was found dead this morning by his wife Shannon." Detective Morris was briefed as he reached the scene of the crime. The doctor's corpse looked almost peaceful lying there on the floor. That is if you ignored the slits on his wrists and throat and the dent in his forehead where it appeared someone had tried to bash his skull in.

"Any suspects yet?"

"None yet, though Detective Jones reckons it was the widow."

"Any reason for that?"

—

"She looks guilty," Detective Jones remarked to his partner as they stood on the other side of the window watching her interview.

"A name like Shannon, doesn't really sound guilty though." Detective Morris countered, he couldn't see it, she seemed distraught to him.

"Her clothes were covered in his blood."

"He was bleeding out all over the floor, of course her clothes are soaked in his blood."

"Fine, I guess we'll have to find some more definitive proof."

"You're that certain she's guilty?" Detective Morris looked at his partner, contemplating the stern lines of his face and the determination in his eyes.

"I sure am."

—

"Shannon's your suspect?" Amelia didn't know what to say. Her neighbours had seemed like such a happy couple. "I can't see her doing such a thing, I mean what reason would she have? They were perfectly happy together, why I never even heard one argument from them."

It was true, their house had always been rather quiet. Perhaps even too quiet, it made Amelia's stomach turn to think of that.

—

"Sir, we're here in regard to your daughter."

Albert tentatively opened the door; he wasn't young anymore and he found himself overly cautious of strangers. He was hardly expecting two police detectives to be standing there. "What about my Shannon?"

"Her husband's been murdered, we wanted to know a bit more about their relationship." One of the officers had a stern, rather grim look to him, but the one asking the question had a kind face.

"Well, they were happy, I mean they never fought... not even after Freddy's accident." Albert felt at ease, as long as he kept his eyes on the nice detective.

"Whose Freddy?" The other officer asked, suspicion in his eyes. He filled Albert with a sense of dread, not so different to how he'd felt the last time officers had been waiting on his doorstep.

"Why my son, Shannon loved her brother dearly. Sadly, he passed away after a motor vehicle accident," It still seemed fresh in Albert's mind, that other day when he'd opened his door to a set of police officers, "Leonard was driving, and they had a crash. Leonard tried to save Freddy with his skills as a doctor and called an ambulance too, but unfortunately my poor Freddy didn't make it. Still Shannon never blamed Leonard, she loved him."

—

"They found the murder weapon."

"Did they?"

Mr Drufflidge didn't really want to tell his client this news, but he supposed it had to be done. "It's a letter opener, and it's covered in your fingerprints."

"So? If it came from my house of course it would have my fingerprints, the killer probably wore gloves. Anyway, I don't have any motive for killing my husband, it's preposterous that anyone could possibly think I did." Mrs Melwet replied briskly.

—

"What is the meaning of this?" Demanded a shocked Shannon Melwet as the detectives' slammed cuffs around her wrists. This was completely unexpected, there should be no reason for them to suspect her let alone arrest her.

"You're under arrest for the murder of your husband, Dr Leonard Melwet." The arresting officer was a stern-faced man, large and brooding, but he couldn't possibly believe she'd done it, could he?

"What? But I didn't have any reason-"

"Freddy Arge, your younger brother who died in a car accident. You blamed Leonard for not being able to save him." It was a soft voice that the other detective used to deliver the statement and read her rights, far too gentle a tone for someone that thought she was guilty.

For a while, she put up a fight and denied everything, certain they'd let her go. Eventually, she grew tired, they weren't relenting, they had no other suspects and were certain of her guilt. It was such a shame she'd ruined that dress all for this, it had always been her favourite dress; that pretty aquamarine until she had dyed it red in her husband's blood.

One Night

A whistling howl fills the room as the door creaks open. Billowing curtains create macabre shapes in the shadows. It sends a chill down Aisha's spine. Instinctively she takes a step back, colliding with Kenneth's chest as she does.

"It's just the wind," Kenneth places a warm hand on her shoulder, squeezing gently before moving in front, "the wind and the dark can play tricks on the mind, we just need to turn on the lights."

Aisha's heart feels as if it could beat right out of her chest as she waits for Kenneth to flick on the lights, but even as she hears the tell-tale click of the switch no light is forthcoming. Her whole being is on edge as the click noise repeats again and again, still no results.

"Old circuitry, I guess nobody's updated the building in a while," Kenneth shrugs, turning to her with a placating smile. "Let's go see if the housekeeper has a candle and some matches, we can borrow."

"We could just go to the motel down the road, they'll have working lights." Aisha mumbles, glancing around the narrow hallway. If she strains her ears, she can just make out the creak of floorboards coming from the other end.

"That's hardly romantic, come on Aisha it's our honeymoon. Haven't you always wanted to stay in a manor house?" Kenneth is all smiles, no tension or fear, it's calming but it doesn't quite dull the nagging concern at the back of Aisha's mind. "It'll be fine, Aisha. It's just for one night."

"Just one." Aisha's voice wobbles a little, she repeats the words trying to instil some sort of courage in herself, "just one night."

"Now, let's go see the housekeeper before she heads off to bed." Kenneth leads her by the arm back to the ornate staircase, down the steps into the parlour.

For a moment Aisha's eyes are transfixed on the front door, heavy oak with delicate carvings of the zodiac and a large brass doorknob. She could run for it, the thought tingles in the back of her mind, they aren't parked far from the door. They could leave right now. The moment passes, Kenneth gently pulling her towards the kitchens.

"Hello, housekeeper?" His voice echoes eerily around the side rooms, but it doesn't seem to faze Kenneth at all. "Hello? We were hoping you might have some candles we could borrow. Hello?"

The echoes unnerve Aisha, goosebumps prickle all along her arms as the noise lingers in her ears. Something about this whole place doesn't feel right. But it's just for one night, she tells herself again and again, just one night. She can survive just one night.

"Hello?" Kenneth releases a sigh of relief, as they press through the doors to the kitchens "Oh good, you're still up."

"Yes, was there something you needed help with?" The elderly houskeeper, almost skin and bones, wears an old-fashioned style of serving garb in off-white with a matching hair cap. Aisha tries not to stare as Kenneth talks to the woman but it's hard not to; three teeth are missing from the front of her mouth, there's an unusual blue tinge to her lips, and her eyes are a wispy grey.

"The lights don't seem to work in our room, I was hoping you'd have some candles and matches we could use." Kenneth seems totally fine talking with her, Aisha's stomach meanwhile twists in knots.

"Ah, yes I should do." The housekeeper smiles a toothy grin before turning from them to rummage in some draws, "Here, these should do you for the night."

She passes them an ornate silver candlestick hosting a set of three large black candles, Aisha takes the offering reluctantly. A shiver passes through her as her hands graze against the old woman's.

"Thank you." Kenneth accepts a box of matches, bowing his head slightly. "We'll be off to bed then, see you in the morning."

"Goodnight." There's a gleam in the housekeeper's eye as she responds which sends another chill down Aisha's spine.

It's just for one night. Aisha tells herself repeatedly as they retrace their steps to the room. Vaguely, she can hear Kenneth talking to her as they walk, but she doesn't take in the words as her ears listen for the creaking of the floorboards at the other end of the hallway. Just one night.

At her insistence, Kenneth leaves the candles burning through the night even as they are ready to sleep. The light gives Aisha a mild sense of reassurance although it conjures many strange shadows to dance along the wooden walls, it's better than complete darkness.

Kenneth falls asleep almost immediately, Aisha cannot. She's too high-strung for sleep just yet, listening to every creak and groan that the house emits. It's all too much, she must try and forget it for the moment. She needs to sleep.

Aisha stares at the candles, watching the flames dance, listening to the barely audible crackle. Slowly she's blocks out the rest of the house from her mind. Her eyes grow heavy as sleep takes her.

Something is wrong.

There's a chill in the air, an emptiness in the bed space beside her, and when she opens her eyes, everything is dark. Her breathing comes fast and panicked, eyes adjusting to the gloom. There's a breeze coming through the window which must have blown out the candles. Aisha tries to wrap herself in logic, to settle her nerves but her panic only deepens as she recalls Kenneth closing the window and locking it in place before they went to bed.

"See no more howling, and now the candles won't go out." Kenneth had said confidently as he latched the window shut. She knows that he wouldn't have gotten up to open it in the night.

Dread twists tight knots in her stomach, whimpering she turns to look beside her to the empty space. Kenneth isn't there. But a deep set of gouge marks are.

There's a loud bang as the window shutters fling further open, the howling wind forces the curtains to billow out almost to the edge of the bed. Aisha lets out a horrified scream before clamping her hands over her mouth.

She can tell the room is empty, but the thought doesn't put her at ease. Aisha doesn't feel alone. It feels as if there are eyes burning holes into her with their gaze, as if somehow, she is being watched. It sets Aisha's hair on end. She must get out, she has to find Kenneth, she can't stay here any longer.

Suppressing a whimper Aisha dips her toes down to the floor, forcing herself past the urge to squeeze her eyes shut and wait for the whole world to just drop away. Biting her bottom lip she looks towards the door, its shape blends into the wall in the darkness but she knows it must be there. The feeling of eyes boring into her back follows her, she moves delicately across the floorboards praying that none of them squeak or crack beneath her weight.

Fingers stretched out before her hoping desperately to find the door she can feel her heart hammering in her chest. Her thoughts bounce back and forth between panicking about escaping and worrying about Kenneth. They should have just gone to Hawaii; she should've insisted more firmly that they stay in the motel.

There's a groan from the floorboards behind her, it takes every ounce of willpower she can muster not to scream. Stifling a sob, she fumbles forward. Her hands find purchase on the door, her left frantically pats along the wood until it grasps the brass doorknob. As the boards continue to groan there's no time for hesitation, Aisha yanks the door open and takes off at a run for the stairs.

Footsteps can be heard coming from both ends of the hallway; loud, slow, and purposeful. Blood is rushing in Aisha's ears, every noise in the house sounds heightened and she can hear a howling wind whistling through the walls. It's too much. She can't take it.

Her right foot catches on the second to last stair but she steadies herself with the railing, not missing a beat, she resumes her dash for the front door. Briefly, a flicker of guilt causes her pause just before the door, she doesn't know where Kenneth is or what's happened to him, but the footsteps are coming ever closer.

Wrenching open the door she dashes for the car, too late recalling she doesn't have the keys. Looking back at the daunting manor house, beautifully haunting in the daylight it is nothing short of menacing in the dark. She tosses up the options; going back into the house to find the keys and perhaps even Kenneth or leaving on foot, dressed only in her lace nightgown.

There are shadows in the open doorway, she can still feel eyes upon her, as a stiff cool breeze sends chills all down her spine. Aisha knows her decision. It is no choice at all, she'd rather face the biting cold of the night than go back inside. Something is in that house, and whatever it is she doesn't want to find out.

Two-Faced

Eve

It was my 16th birthday. I was finally going to meet my twin. I could hardly wait as the last minutes on the clock ticked by.

21:54

21:55

21:56

It was time. Excitedly pressing my right thumb against the mirror, a set of green concentric circles flickered and stretched across the reflective surface casting a dull glow over my blue skin. I held my breath waiting for the surface to go from reflective to clear; I wonder what will she look like?

"It's about time!" A sharp, commanding voice snapped as the mirror rippled into its monitor state. In front of me, I saw someone who was practically my double, not surprising as we were meant to be identical but still, it was one thing to know something and another altogether to see it.

"Hi," I tried my hardest not to stutter and made full eye contact which is how I noticed our first difference, "your eyes are purple."

"Yes, I suppose they are today. You know it's pretty rude to just comment on somebody's eyes?"

"Sorry, sorry. Uh, let's start over. I'm Eve, it's a pleasure to finally meet you."

"Scout. And I suppose it's okay meeting you. Honestly, though I'm surprised you connected."

"Are you? I mean why wouldn't I? I've always wanted to meet you, Scout!" She didn't hold eye contact with me, rather she seemed to be scanning the room.

"Why?" When she did look at me it was piercingly sharp. There was a ferocity to her stare.

"Well, you're my twin."

"So? Everyone has a twin, it's standard Scilun biology, you know that." Scout tutted and clicked her tongue against her teeth.

"I mean of course, but that doesn't take away our connection! I guess I just always wanted to know what you were like, if we're the same or different? And what's it like being part of the Gemini System?"

"Ah, there it is. You just wanted to know what it's like to be confined within GS. It's *fine*, I guess. What's it like being in the real world?" Her gaze shifted from me to the emblem on my uniform "What's school like?"

"Oh, um it's good. You don't have school in the Gemini System?"

"No, why would we? GS is a virtual system; we have no need for anything because we don't physically exist anymore. If I want to learn something I just ask, and the system provides information. Come on, you know all this, surely, they teach you all about it in *school*." There was venom in the way she said school. I felt bad about not changing out of my uniform, but I'd been so excited to finally meet my twin.

"I suppose they do, but it's pretty vague and I just thought you'd have a different perspective." I'd focused my gaze on the floor brushing my foot back and forth along the tiles, "It's getting late, I better head to bed..."

"Right, because you need sleep." Scout scoffed at me just before the feed cut out.

Alone, staring at my own reflection I bit my lip. It hadn't gone how I had hoped but maybe she'd just been having a bad day I told myself. I forced a smile at my reflection, my big orange eyes stared straight back at me as I took a deep breath, tomorrow I was sure would definitely be better.

--

"Brenda, can I ask you a question?" Straining to keep up with my friend's fast pace on the track, my voice came out as a wheeze.

"Of course, Eve, what are best friends for?" She'd smiled, noticeably slowing down for me.

"When you turned 16 last month, did you access the Gemini System? Did you talk to your twin?" It was hard to get out my words without gasping.

"As if I could resist!" Brenda wiped a small fleck of sweat from her turquoise brow.

"What was it like?"

"Why? Not sure if you want to talk to your twin?"

"No, I met her yesterday. I'm just curious about how it was for you." I was always amazed how Brenda could seemingly multi-task whilst running, while I remained barely able to talk.

"Oh. Well, it was great. Really shocking of course, my twin and I are fraternal and that's about all Mum would tell me before I met them. Turns out they're a he, it was really weird but after a few minutes chatting it was fantastic. He's really interesting; we talk every weekend."

"I see. I wish I could be that close to my twin."

"You can, and you will just give it time." She flashed me one more smile before picking back up her pace, "Don't worry about it Eve, you're so sweet she's bound to like you."

Brenda was gone in an instant which was good in a way as it let me slow down just a little, I'd never be able to keep up with her properly. But at least I'd gotten some perspective; it was weird at first for Brenda too so surely it would get better.

--

As soon as I got home, I changed out of my uniform, school seemed to be a sore spot for Scout so I tried for something neutral. The thin black dress looked fairly unassuming as I stood in front of the mirror. Taking a deep breath I pressed my thumb to the glass.

"Back again?" Scout's right eye ridge raised as she spoke.

"I think we got off on the wrong foot yesterday. I'd really like to get to know you, so can we please give this another shot?" I gave her my biggest smile, hoping my dimples were showing.

"Alright, fine if you are so eager to know me." She regarded me with a rather withering look, perhaps she was being sarcastic?

"Excellent!" If she was it didn't really matter to me, I wanted to press forward and be her friend no matter what. "So you can request information and learn at will, what's the strangest thing you've learnt?"

"That squid on Oya 3 have basically the same genetic code to us Sciluns, with a few small variations of course. Next question." Just like the day before, her eyes were more focused on the room then on me, but trying to make firm eye contact with her I noticed something different.

"Your eyes are green?"

"And?"

"Yesterday they were purple."

"One of the perks here in GS is that I can change my physical appearance to a degree at will. Watch." As she talked her eyes slowly changed hue before settling into a soft pink shade. "Of course, they don't want us to be completely unrecognisable to you physical people, so we're restricted to cosmetic changes. Our base appearance is created from a predictability module of our family line. Much easier for the programmers when we're meant to be identical twins."

"Oh, I see." I don't know why it seemed so strange to me but I suppose I'd never really thought of the twins inside the Gemini System as anything but normal. Obviously, that wasn't the case as after all they only exist as souls—conscious minds—within a virtual world.

"Next question," Scout said rousing me from my thoughts.

"Do you have friends?"

"Why do you care?"

"I just want to know. Maybe your friends are twins of my friends, wouldn't that be cool?" I could feel myself grinning, but Scout's expression was set in a firm frown, it was somewhat disconcerting given our practically identical appearance.

"Not really. I know some people but in here it isn't really like there's much use for bonding. I mean we can't physically interact or procreate so we hold very little use for each other."

"But don't you get lonely?"

"Not a bit." Scout turned away from me. "My turn, what are our parents like?"

"Oh, they're great! Mum's really fantastic at making stuff and Dad's just amazing at cooking, I'm hoping to learn some of his recipes soon." I wondered what she could be staring at, I tried to peer past her but everything in the mirror besides her was just black and white lines. "What are you looking at?"

"I'm checking the files on Mum and Dad." She looked back at me, "What else would I be looking at?"

I shrugged in response.

"Oh, I get it, you thought perhaps there was actually a room or something that I was in. You think there's stuff to look at here. Well, there isn't, it's a virtual world I can fill it with whatever I like, or I can leave it empty. Mostly I leave it empty."

"I, uh, see." I murmured, "Well, uh, did you have any more questions for me?"

"Not today."

The monitor rippled before the feed cut out. Once more I was alone staring at my reflection. Perhaps tomorrow we'll become friends?

Scout

Eve's annoying blue face dissolved into fragments of code as I terminated the connection. At least I had that much freedom. I might have been at her beck and call for conversations but at least I could choose when to end them. It was frustrating how she kept trying to make friends, just because we're twins doesn't mean she's entitled to my friendship... especially not when she had the gall to pretend she was ignorant of my circumstances.

"And what's it like being part of the Gemini System?" Her irksome question from yesterday had rattled in my thoughts, if I'd had real skin, I'm sure it would have crawled.

The Gemini System, the miracle answer to the Scilun overpopulation problem. I wasn't naïve enough to let the propaganda fool me, sure it solved overpopulation, but it was no miracle.

"Computer, bring up appearance options!" Ever since the link initiated between Eve and me, I'd felt uncomfortable with my appearance, I found it unsettling to look at her and see my own face as if I was just a flawed copy of her.

"Here are the options for appearance change, Scout." The mechanical voice chimed all around me as the space directly in front of me morphed into a display screen.

Skin Colour: N/A- identical protocol

Height: N/A-identical protocol

Appendages: N/A-identical protocol

"Urgh," I scrolled past option after option, trying to find the available ones. "Computer, hide unavailable options and display only available options!"

An opal-coloured cube rolled across the display banishing almost all the appearance options from sight. I glowered at the screen which presented me with the same three options it always did.

Eye colour: Orange, Green, Purple, Black, White, Yellow, Blue, Red or Pink

Piercings: Hearing Appendages - 0, 1, 2, 3, 4 or 5. Abdominal Appendages - 0 or 1. Eyelids - 0, 1 or 2. Nasal Appendage - 0, 1 or 2.

Reset to perfectly identical.

I couldn't help but snort at the last option, being an exact duplicate of Eve was exactly what I didn't want. However, piercings didn't exactly hold much point in GS... nothing really did, it was all just code made to simulate some sort of reality—a consolation prize for being the unlucky twins condemned to a virtual existence for the sake of managing population numbers. That said maybe it'd be worth applying piercings just to freak her out, I was willing to bet Eve would never disfigure her pretty visage.

--

She'd screamed when she saw me, her face paled a little and I chuckled. The coding for the maximum number of piercings had rendered my face a horrifying site but it was easily undoable and so worth it for making Eve's skin crawl.

"Scout, you uh changed your look quite a bit." For the first time in our brief acquaintance, she was the one avoiding my gaze, I levelled her with my best stare trying to pin her in place with my eyes as she nervously jostled from left foot to right foot.

"Yeah, I thought I'd try something new."

"Oh, um of course." Eve's gaze lowered to the floor; an expression of guilt smeared across her face.

"So, what questions do you have for me today, twin?" I smirked as her gaze remained firmly on the floor.

"No questions, not really, I've got some photos of Mum and Dad... I just thought you might like to see them?" She'd timidly raised her head and peered at me ever so slightly.

I'd fought against the urge to scoff and bite my lip, why would I ever want to see the photos she had? Was she trying to rub it in that she physically existed, while I was simply a consciousness shackled to this banal virtual reality?

"Sure," I forced myself to say instead of erupting at her.

"Oh, great!" She smiled that sickening sweet smile she gave me the first time she activated our connection, and if I was real I'm sure I would have puked. "Here's one from their wedding, it's really old but don't you just love Mum's tri-coloured dress?"

"I'm not big on fashion." I quipped and she rapidly put down the picture.

"This is one from my primary education graduation!" Excitedly she had pressed the next image right into the monitor, affronting my vision with a tiny version of her and our parents. "I had a lot of difficulties in primary education so they were really relieved when I managed to graduate with my friends."

"I didn't think you could fail primary education."

"It's not common but it is possible," Eve whispered her response as she removed the image. "And this is one Dad gave me to show you, it's him and Mum in the birthing chambers with you and me as babies."

Seething hot rage threatened to overtake me as I looked on at the image she held up. It contained within it what must be one of the only pieces of evidence of my long since destroyed physical body.

"Tear that up!" I couldn't look at it anymore, I couldn't look at *her* anymore, I turned away from the monitor. "Tear it up and burn the fragments, I never want to see it again!"

"Scout?"

"I mean it, tear it up! Then do me a favour and never speak to me again!" I whipped back around to pierce her with one last glare— if I wasn't just a consciousness, if this wasn't just some code based appearance then I'm sure I'd have had tears in my eyes.

"Scou-"

I terminated the connection then before she could utter another word, I was done with this torment.

Eve

"-out" The feed cut out before I could finish calling out her name. That had just been a complete disaster. "I didn't mean to upset you." I whispered the end of my sentence and pressed my hand to the mirror.

I was such an idiot. Hot, painful tears pricked at my eyes as a loud sob wrenched itself from my chest.

"Eve, sweetie are you okay?" Dad's melodic voice called through the door to me as another sob racked my body. "Eve, I'm going to come in okay?"

I didn't want Dad to come in but words wouldn't form in my throat, all I managed in response was a groan.

"Eve?" I curled myself into a ball on the floor, not wanting to look into Dad's big yellow eyes. "Sweetie, what happened?"

He placed a three-fingered hand on my shoulder and squeezed gently. I felt so stupid crying there on the floor, so incredibly stupid. I should have at least gone to my room before breaking down, at least then I could have had some privacy.

"Is something wrong?" Mum quickly arrived to add to my suffering.

"Clearly, though I'm not sure what." Dad replied.

"Oh, Eve, you know you can always talk to us about what's wrong?" I could hear Mum approaching, as far as I was concerned it couldn't get any worse.

Her soft stubby fingers tickled under my chin, as I scrunched my eyes shut tighter she traced slow figures of eight along my neck. My body no longer capable of ignoring it shuddered before a small laugh split from my lips and my eyes forced themselves open. Mum's orange eyes had twinkled back at me, a smug smile on her lips.

"There, now why don't you tell Mum and Dad what the problem is?"

"I don't want to," I could feel the puffiness in my eyes, the wet slick of tears not yet dried on my cheeks. "I'm fine."

"You're not. Now, please tell us what's brought this on all of a sudden? You're usually such a happy and upbeat girl." Mum's eyes seemed to pierce straight into the depths of my soul, how did she do that?

"Scout hates me," I mumbled, half wanting to tell them and half wanting to keep it to myself and let my upset fester like a wound.

"Why would she hate you? She's your twin, I'm sure she doesn't hate you." A squeeze on the shoulder from Dad accompanied Mum's words.

"It's nothing, I don't want to talk about it." I pushed Dad's hand off my shoulder and scrambled up off the floor, avoiding eye contact with mum. "Just leave it."

"Eve, I'm sure she doesn't hate you. You're twins, you have a connection." Mum reached for me, but I pushed her hands away, finally my eyes had settled on the photograph. It'd fallen to the ground, so I bent to snatch it up, shrugging off Mum and Dad's words of comfort.

"All Sciluns have twins! There's nothing special about us being twins!" I muttered as I tore up the photo before shouldering past Mum and Dad. "I'm going to bed."

--

They were wrong, she definitely hated me. I thumbed at the mini monitor that Mum bought for me.

"This way if she reaches out, you'll be able to tell no matter where you are because you'll always have a mirror surface on hand."

I had told her it was a waste of credits, mini monitors were only worthwhile if you and your twin communicated frequently, but she wouldn't listen.

Technically I could have reached out to her, but she'd seemed pretty clear that she wanted nothing to do with me and I didn't want to abuse her right to privacy. Still, I had wished I could talk to her and apologise properly.

Scout

Every day I would change my appearance, I couldn't seem to settle on anything because nothing made me look different enough from her. Everything had been just fine until she insisted on rubbing her physical form, her stake in reality, in my face.

Maybe some people were content with their fate as part of the GS but I was sick of it, tired of being tethered to an eternal emptiness. Why did I have to be the twin stuck in here? *Why?* That's was actually a good question.

"Computer, requesting information access on how it is decided which twin goes into GS."

A small ping that emanated from all directions at once notified me that my request had been lodged because, of course, it couldn't just be public access. I wondered if schools briefed them about this stuff, or if they truly just fed the propaganda. Mere moments later, a secondary ping told me my request had been accepted, the space before me transformed into a long-winded read-out.

Gemini System candidates are determined based on health scans, in the case that neither twin is healthier a random selection is initiated.

The line grabbed my interest immediately, but left me with another question.

"Computer, requesting health scan readouts for myself and Eve at time of birth."

"Information coming on display."

A series of cubes dissolved the government papers and replaced my vision with a health form, it had less writing on it than I expected.

Eve: Healthy, no abnormalities detected.

Scout: Healthy, no abnormalities detected.

I felt my anger bubbling over, so that was it, there was no reason? We were so perfectly identical that even our health scans had come out the same.

"Ha, ha, ha." If I'd had physical mass I probably would have done something silly like stumble backwards and fall on my butt like in videos, but I was part of the GS so I didn't have physical mass. I didn't have anything. Laughter peeled out of me in short bursts.

I caught myself soon enough, collected myself and channelled my upset into anger. After all; laughter, my voice, none of it was real. I was merely a disconnected consciousness stuck within a digital framework the only real thing about me was my thoughts. And right then all of those were angry because there should at least have been a reason for why I was shoved into here instead of *her*.

--

It's always seemed kind of pointless but now that I had some glimpse of what I was missing out on it seemed all the more agonisingly unbearable. I wanted to live and experience the world, but instead, was forced to be a reflection at her beck and call. The only bright side was she seemed to have listened to me and I'd been blissfully free of her for a month.

Some of the other occupants suggested I read the news feeds, they said it helped them feel connected to the real world but it just made me feel even more disconnected.

Cruises between Oya 1 and Oya 3 have been cancelled due to a large number of comets passing through the region. I'd bet interspace travel was interesting, seeing how the different atmospheres affect Scilun physiology, having the physiology to monitor the effects.

Gemini System becoming overcrowded for memory banks, optional erasure to be offered to inhabitants. Oh, joy, at least the older members of this drab space would finally be able to move on—I couldn't imagine they'd offer it to younger inhabitants.

Scientists create a device to switch active consciousness of physical form with the consciousness of twin stored in Gemini System.

Squid on Oya 3 being used to advance medical research. Wait a minute, I thought.

"Computer, cycle back to that last headline!"

Scientists create a device to switch active consciousness of physical form with the consciousness of twin stored in Gemini System.

"I didn't just imagine it then." My eyes greedily scanned the data.

A group of scientists on Oya 2 have manufactured a device that allows the swap of consciousness. The device is in the last stages of testing and will provide a way to switch out those considered a risk to themselves and/or Scilun society with their twin in the Gemini System (GS). The twin within GS will have to be tested first to ensure that the switch is for the best.

This would be it, my way into reality.

Eve

"You have a contact request!" The dull voice of the mini-monitor computer announced, slicing through my boredom.

I'd been staring at the ceiling for half an hour, it'd become a kind of habit to just stare off at nothing whilst leaving my mind blank. Dad said it was unhealthy to stay cooped up doing nothing but that's all I'd wanted to do.

"Who from?" I couldn't even be bothered to look at the monitor, it was just an annoying reminder of the one person who hated me with all their being.

"Scout."

"Wait, who?"

"Scout." The computer repeated her name once more for me, but I was still in disbelief.

"Why would she contact me?"

"Unknown."

"Ugh!" Sometimes the computer in the monitor could be so frustrating, obviously, I didn't expect it to know why out of the blue she'd decided I was worth talking to. "Fine, whatever, patch her through."

"Finger scan needed."

"Right, of course." I rolled over and leaned across the bed to grab hold of the monitor, flipping it open I pressed my right thumb to the surface and watched as the circles pulsed on the screen before fading away. "Come on, this is taking forever." As I complained at the monitor about the wait I noticed something odd, I could swear my reflection had just blinked. "Scout?"

A thin smile played across the face in the reflection as big orange eyes stared piercingly into my own.

"It is you, isn't it, Scout?"

A moment of silence seemed to drag on forever as I held my breath waiting for the reflection to respond. She'd laughed.

"Wow, you should see your face... Oh wait I can show you," she pulled a face that I could only assume was meant to mimic my own expression.

"You look different." Was all I could manage to say.

"I look like you, that's what you mean isn't it? It's not like it's hard, all I had to do was request my appearance be reset to identical and voila I'm an exact copy of you."

"I thought you didn't want to look like me,"

"Oh I don't, but the way I see it I don't look like you, *you* look like me."

"I see. So... what did you want to talk to me about?" It was foolish but I couldn't help but hope this would be the start of a turnaround, that we'd finally be friends.

"Tell me all about living. What's it like to breath? How does walking feel? All of it." Her determined expression had sent a small shiver down my spine.

"Well it's kind of hard to describe breathing, but walking is nice unless you do too much of it and then your legs hurt. And changing your appearance is really difficult *here*," I forced myself to focus on what I was saying, I didn't want to say the wrong thing and offend Scout again. "You can't just decide you want to look different from day to day, and a lot of the ways that you can go about an appearance change really hurt... but ear piercings aren't that bad." I tilted my head a little to try show Scout my piercings, one in each ear.

"Huh, I didn't realise you had earrings." She tilted her own head in response showing bare unmarked ears. "Tell me more about living."

"Okay!" I beamed at her through the mini monitor. "What would you like to know next?"

--

I could feel a yawn coming on, Scout and I had talked for hours the night before and whilst I was happy we were finally connecting it seems to be at the detriment of my grades.

"Eve, are you okay?" Brenda waved a turquoise hand in front of my face and her small jewel-like ruby eyes peered into mine.

"I'm fine," I'd averted my gaze from hers, "just pretty sure I failed today's test is all."

"Failed? Eve, are you sure you're fine?" She knitted her brow at me.

"Yeah, I just need to get a little more sleep, but I don't want to offend Scout by cutting off our conversations too early."

"You're talking to your twin again?"

"Mmm, we've been speaking again for about a week now. Sorry, I should have told you."

"No, it's fine. It's just you suddenly stopped talking to her and went all gloomy, I'm worried you're investing too much of yourself into connecting with her."

"Brenda, she's my twin I want to be close to her." I did my best to give Brenda a big grin without yawning, "I just need to find a balance between talking to her and getting enough rest for school."

Brenda gave me a questioning look before returning to her work. But I remember feeling that she really shouldn't worry, it would all be fine, I'd tell Scout I couldn't have such long conversations anymore as I needed to focus on my studies—she'd understand.

Scout

She couldn't be onto me, Eve wasn't the type to be distrusting. This was just a sign that my plan was working. Getting her grades to drop was just the first relatively easy step, given how trusting she was, and if she wouldn't stay up to talk to me then it was time to roll out phase two. Though it'd taken a lot of obscure searching I was fairly sure I'd gotten a good grasp on how to do it—to really sink under her skin.

"Computer, I'd like to see the appearance options please." In a second the long list of options had been brought in front of me. "Just the piercing options, specifically ear-based options, please." The digital cube rolled across the landscape quickly erasing all the other options from view.

I didn't really need to look over the list of options; I already knew exactly what I wanted.

Eve

I peered into the bathroom, it was blissfully empty so I rushed to the sink twisted the cold tap on and scooped handfuls of water up to pour over my face. The cool splash of water on my face had been exactly what I needed after running non-stop for the better part of an hour.

I watched the slow trickle of water droplets tracing a path down from my forehead to the tip of my nose in the mirror. Following a single droplet's journey in the mirror I'd let out a heavy sigh, my grades hadn't been improving and Scout had seemed oddly aloof lately.

My conversation with Mum and Dad that morning had replayed in the back of my mind.

"You need to focus, Eve. If your grades continue to drop, you'll be held back." Dad huffed as he cooked breakfast.

"Sweetie, you've really been worrying us lately. You just haven't seemed yourself, and now your grades are suffering... Maybe you should see somebody?" Mum had chimed as she laid the table.

"Or perhaps we should get you a tutor?"

"No. I'll get my grades back up. I've just been spending a lot of time with Scout and haven't gotten enough rest, but I'm going to do better. I promise." They'd both given me worrying looks then.

"Well if they don't improve a little this week we'll have to restrict your contact, and confiscate your mini-monitor." Mum nodded along to Dad's suggestion as if cutting me off from my twin was no big deal.

"Okay," I mumbled in defeat, I should have said something more.

I shook my head, there was no point dwelling on a conversation I'd already lost. Another splash of water on my face, I looked back at the mirror once more and forced a smile to try pepping myself back up.

"All right, Eve. Time to go ace a test." Just as I'd been about to turn the door handle something had nagged at my mind; was my reflection dry? I'd turned back to look at the mirror, but nothing seemed off, "You're just imagining things, Eve. Come on you need to go work on getting those grades up."

--

There it was again. I'd been noticing an odd flicker in my reflection, and sometimes I could swear she'd blink when I didn't or wink at me. It'd become considerably more noticeable since Dad confiscated my mini-monitor and installed a parental lockout to keep me from access-ing the Gemini System.

The flicker occurred once more and this time I was fairly certain she was smiling, and I most certainly wasn't. I dragged my fingers down my face, stretching my skin unflatteringly, the reflection was definitely smiling. "Ugh, I wish I could talk to Scout about this."

There had been a chuckle at that, I almost hadn't heard it but the room was otherwise completely quiet.

"Now I really am going crazy. Come on, Eve, time to get to bed." I shook off the odd sensation the noise had left tingling in my spine, maybe I just needed to get some rest. I took one last glance in the mirror, my reflection remained still holding my gaze with her identical orange eyes. Her eyes might be my own but I could swear there was something insidious to my reflection, the looks she gave me sometimes made me feel as if she wished to do me harm... But that was crazy, or maybe it wasn't.

Scout

"Incoming call!" The mechanical voice blared at me.

"Wait, hold on just a minute." The computer didn't listen to me and even as I protested a display opened up directly in front of me. "Well, this is a surprise."

"Hello, Scout."

"Hi Mum and Dad," Of course my parents could contact me, I'd heard as much from other GS citizens, but it begged the question, "to what do I owe this pleasure?"

"We're calling about Eve." I tried to maintain a straight face, there was no need for concern. "She's been distant and moody lately, and that's not like her at all."

"Her grades are slipping, even with all her distractions removed..." Mum chimed in as Dad levelled me with an accusatory look, but neither of them said it so I gave them a push.

"And?"

"And the only recent significant change in her life has been talking with you, Scout." Dad jumped on the bait, and I held back a sigh of relief—nobody had caught on to me yet.

"So, you think I'm the problem." I took a defensive tone making sure to avert my gaze from them and look hurt, I changed my tone to be ever so slightly sadder. "Maybe you just haven't been paying attention. Eve's always been a little disconnected, at least as long as we've been talking. She doesn't really enjoy school, and she's so curious about GS it's almost like she wishes she didn't have to be a part of reality."

They were taken aback, I could tell from their facial expressions, but they didn't give away anything else.

"Thank you for your opinion, Scout." Mum had said just as the feed cut out. If I'd had a real body or somebody was watching I might have bit my lip, I was on difficult terrain. There was nothing to do now but bide my time.

--

Mum and Dad didn't call again, but I still needed to be careful not to tip my hand. Slowly unravelling Eve's sanity was a precision task, I had to time every movement carefully whilst being cautious not to make my strikes too frequently. It would be a real wrench in the works if somebody picked up on what I was doing, after all, GS was meant to be un-hackable—but that was from the outside.

Eve

Mum and Dad were seriously concerned, I could hear them whispering when I wasn't in the room. They thought I was losing it. Even I thought I was losing it sometimes. As I'd entered the shower I'd averted my gaze from the mirror, trying to focus on anything else in the room.

I couldn't be going mad. The water rushed over me like a waterfall as I contemplated my circumstances, gaze firmly trained on the tiles.

"Think Eve, think. There has to be some logical explanation, you're not going insane so there has to be something afoot." I was drenched as I exited the shower. "Mirrors can't hurt you, they're just a reflective surface. There must be something you aren't seeing, Eve."

When I looked into the mirror, I saw the flicker and there was a distinctive smugness to my reflection's grin, it kind of reminded me of Scout. But I told myself the Gemini System didn't work like that, it was only accessible from reality via bio scans, so it couldn't be Scout. Or could it?

"Scout, is that you?" I whispered, leaning in towards the mirror. The corners of my reflection's mouth twitched but there was no answer. "Scout?" I pressed my hand to the mirror and when my reflection didn't raise her hand, I was certain. "It is you."

She didn't say anything, but a wicked smile crossed her face as she made a shushing motion at me.

"You've been spying on me? Why? How?" As she continued to remain silent my voice raised in pitch until finally, I was yelling at her, "Why are you doing this? SCOUT?"

The mirror had flickered again just before Mum and Dad barged in, as I was mid-sentence Mum grabbed my shoulders to spin me around.

"Eve, what are you doing?"

"I'm talking to Scout, she's been watching me through the mirrors! I want answers," I pulled against Mum's grip, I had to get back to the mirror.

"That's nonsense, Eve. You can't be talking to Scout, she can't watch you through the mirrors, that's not how GS works." Mum shook my shoulders as Dad ushered her to pull me out of the room, all the while I strained to reach the mirror. "Besides you're locked out, there isn't any way for you to contact her."

"But she can. She *is*. I know it!" As they pulled me from the room I could see the flicker and my reflection betrayed me with a sinister grin. It was like a gut punch. How could she be so two-faced? More so, what was her plan... what was going to happen to me?

--

The clinic my parents brought me to smelt like too much chemical cleaner had been used and the doctors were all giving me odd looks. What was that place?

"Eve, if you could just lean back in the chair." I'd flicked my gaze to the left where a doctor stood in a long lab coat, "This will only take a second, and it won't hurt a bit."

As I leaned back, they lowered a large metal device over my head. It emitted an odd electronic hum and as the sound increased, I was left with one thought, they lied.

--

"Eve, wait up!" A pesky voice called *her* name from behind me. "Eve!" A tight grip fell upon my left shoulder, and I almost crumpled to the ground. "Eve, where have you been? I didn't see you all break."

I turned to face them; her turquoise skin glimmered with a sheen of sweat in the sunlight. Taking a deep breath, I fixed my orange eyes on her ruby ones in a hard stare.

"Sorry, Eve's gone." I nod to her hand on my shoulder, "I'm Scout, could you kindly please remove your vice grip?"

"Eve? What happened to you?"

"Nothing happened to Eve. She's happy now, and I'm here." I forced a curt smile for the stranger, "Now I really must be getting a move on, I'd hate to be late for my first day of *school*."

Acknowledgments

This collection is dedicated to my family, as it was when I first released it as a much smaller collection available only as an ebook on Amazon in 2017. However, a lot has changed in my life over the past five years and my writing has (I believe) grown to be all the better for it. So, it would feel disingenuous not to acknowledge the people who have helped support and encourage me in the time since I first released *The Short Story Press Collection*.

Firstly, I must thank my mother, without her help I would not have been able to bring this collection into print. She has supported me and my brother our whole lives, encouraging me to pursue my dreams and keep at it even when I've been scared and overcome with anxiety about what the future may hold. All my family have supported me, but she's been the biggest supporter of them all.

In the vein of support, I would be amiss not to mention some of my closest friends; Asha, Kate, Melissa, Taisla, and a few others (I'm sorry if you don't see your name here, but I trust those of you know who you are). These friends have been kind enough to buy copies of my works, to ask for my autograph, to encourage me when I need it, and to listen to my concerns. A special mention also goes to my friend Tim who gives me prompts for writing that I post on my blog for the Wednesday Prompt Smash, some of which have been expanded and found their way into this collection. Truly I am so lucky in life to have found such wonderful friends.

There are other friends I'd like to acknowledge, those who are fellow members of the writing community (whether they are published yet or not). I've had the pleasure these last few years of meeting many other emerging writers and making valuable friendships amongst my peers, a step I don't think I'd have had the courage to take if not for Alanah Andrews (*Eve of Eridu*) posting in the Fiction Writers Facebook group about wanting to create a group for Australian and New Zealand, speculative fiction writers. Thanks to Alanah putting together Aussie Speculative Fiction I was able to interact more with the writing community, and from that, I made some wonderful friends including Austin P. Sheehan (*Submerged City*), Marcus Turner (*Tides of War*), S.M. Isaac (*River of Diamonds*), and Kel E. Fox (*Darkhaven*) along with many others.

S.M. Isaac and Kel E. Fox in particular are dear friends, we have a small private group along with a few other wonderful writing friends that do daily-ish check-ins and help keep each other accountable as well as provide encouragement, advice and support. And for the last few years, we've also done a Secret Santa amongst us.

I'd be remiss if I forgot to mention my fellow Brisbane and Queensland-based writers. In 2021 as Covid restrictions lifted I made the trip to Brisbane to meet in person with an eclectic and delightful group of writers. A group that meets once a month for coffee and a chat, where we can discuss personal matters as well as our writing; I always walk away with a new book recommendation. Over this past year, I have felt so much love and support from my fellow Brissie writers; from some of them sharing social media posts about my novel *It's All Magic To Me* to simply being asked how I am doing and being listened to without judgment. Each and every member of our Brisbane writing crew has been so welcoming, and I adore them all (I've got a stack of books to read through by different members too), and it's all thanks to G.D. Ison who organised getting us together. A special thank you also goes to Ray See who invited me along in the first place, it was such a delight to be considered and is so much fun every time I attend. I can't list everyone here but I'd like to include Nicole Melanson, Ky Garvey, James Maasdorp, Alex Dupriez, Michelle Upton, and Liv Dunford. Sorry to all those I didn't mention but I appreciate you all.

There's one more person I'd like to acknowledge and that's my boyfriend, Ryan. We've been together almost two years at the time I'm bringing this to print. He has been such a comfort this past year; helping me and my family move between rental homes as we wait for repairs to finish on our house, picking me up from Brisbane after writer meet-ups, mentioning my books and my writing to his friends and students, encouraging me to follow my dreams. I honestly, truly hope we will have many more years together, supporting each other's dreams.

Lastly, Miley and Akela, my dogs, they can't read, and they certainly don't always prove helpful towards writing but they do wonders for my mental health. Plus, I'd feel bad if I didn't mention them when they are such a big, important part of my life.

About the Author

Sasha Hanton grew up living in the tropics of Darwin, Northern Territory (Larrakia Country). From a young age, she devoured books and iced coffee, both of which she continues to intake on an almost daily basis. Now living on beautiful Bribie Island in Queensland (Gubbi Gubbi Country) her time is split between writing and spoiling her dogs, Miley and Akela.

Sasha, who has a Bachelor of Journalism from Bond University, has dabbled in the journalistic profession but finds fiction far more fascinating. Coming from a multicultural background (Eurasian) she aspires to make her writing inclusive for people from all walks of life and to bring a unique blend of eastern and western culture to her writing.

Throughout her life, she has been a lover of history and mythology and frequently finds some way to worm one or the other into her storytelling. When she's not writing or reading, she can be found walking her dogs and volunteering.

Other Works
It's All Magic To Me
Customerpocalypse

Featured in Anthologies
Dealt in Sin - Beginnings from Deadset Press
Fae Deal – Faeries from Iron Faerie Publishing
Uncovering the Seal – Fire and Brimstone from Specul8 Publishing
Shift – Stories of Hope from Deadset Press